MONSTER MENACE

SCOOBY-DOO & THE MONSTER MENACE

ISBN 1 84023 999 9

Published by Titan Books, a division of
Titan Publishing Group Ltd.
144 Southwark St
London SE1 0UP

SCRIPT: Earl Kress, Brett Lewis, Alex Simmons, Rurik Tyler
PENCILS: Leo Batic, Vincent Deporter, Joe Staton, Anthony Williams
INKS: Jeff Albrecht, Ryan Cline, Dave Hunt, Horatio Ottolini, Andrew Pepoy
LETTERS: John Constanza, Sergio Garcia, Nick J. Nap
COLOURS: Paul Becton, Digital Chameleon, Sno Cone

A CIP catalogue record for this title is available from the British Library.

First edition: February 2005

10 9 8 7 6 5 4 3 2 1

Printed in Italy.

What did you think of this book? We love to hear from our readers. Please email us at: readerfeedback@titanemail.com, or write to us at the above address. You can also visit us at www.titanbooks.com

WOW! THIS ISLAND RESORT IS BEAUTIFUL!
DID YOU KNOW "ALOHA" MEANS BOTH HELLO AND GOODBYE?
Aloha HOTEL
LIKE, WOW! WHAT A FRIENDLY PLACE! LOOKS LIKE THE WHOLE TOWN IS COMING TO GREET US!
AAAGGGHHHH!!!
HOW'S IT GOING? PLEASED TO MEET YOU! LIKE, WHERE'S THE FOOD?
RELLO! RELLO! RELLO!
THEY DON'T SEEM TO BE RUNNING TOWARDS US AS MUCH AS RUNNING AWAY FROM SOMETHING!
THEY WERE ALL SCREAMING! MAYBE THERE'S A CELEBRITY ON THE OTHER SIDE OF THE ISLAND!
CREATURE FROM THE BLUE LAGOON
EARL KRESS..........WRITER
ANTHONY WILLIAMS......PENCILLER
JEFF ALBRECHT..........INKER
SERGIO GARCIA..........LETTERER
PAUL BECTON..........COLORIST
DIGITAL CHAMELEON..SEPARATOR
HARVEY RICHARDS.....ASST EDITOR
JOAN HILTY..........EDITOR

RAGGY... REAWEED!
ROARRRRRRR!
ZOINKS! LIVING SEAWEED!
CHATTER! CHATTER!
POINK!
SEAWEED? LIKE, THEY'RE MY FAVORITE SURF AND TURF BOY BAND!
THE SEAWEED'S NOT ALIVE...
...BUT THE CREATURE UNDER IT IS!
HEAD FOR THE ALOHA HOTEL!
AND IN THIS CASE, ALOHA MEANS "GOODBYE, CREATURE!"
GANGWAY!
REAH! RANGRAY!

I HATE TOURIST SEASON!
I HATE CREATURE SEASON!
AH, YOU ALL MUST BE MYSTERY, INC.!
I'M AL O. HA, MANAGER OF THE ALOHA HOTEL. I SENT FOR YOU!
ALOHA, HA! ha, ha, ha!
WE ALREADY SAW WHY YOU CALLED US!
WHAT IS THIS BIG FISH TALE?
"WELL, KIDS, THE ISLAND OF PUKASHELLI AND THE ALOHA HOTEL HAS BEEN A POPULAR TOURIST DESTINATION FOR MANY YEARS!
"NOT TOO LONG AGO, THE ISLAND WAS BOUGHT BY AWARD- WINNING ACTOR MAURICE ORSON. THEY SAY HE'S LIVING ON THE OTHER SIDE OF THE ISLAND, BUT WE NEVER SEE HIM!
"THEN, A FEW WEEKS AGO, THE CREATURE AROSE FROM THE LAGOON AND BEGAN TERRORIZING THE TOURISTS!
"HE'S DRIVING ALL MY BUSINESS AWAY!"
AND I SAY GOOD RIDDANCE! TOURISTS ARE NOTHING BUT TROUBLE!
WE'LL SEE WHAT WE CAN FIND OUT, MR. HA!
I'LL BE IN MY OFFICE IF YOU NEED ME!

DAPHNE, VELMA AND I WILL TALK TO THE REST OF THE HOTEL STAFF. SHAGGY, YOU AND SCOOBY GO OUTSIDE AND SEE WHAT YOU CAN TURN UP!
I HOPE WE TURN UP A BUFFET! LIKE, I'M STARVED!
RUMBLE!
GRUMBLE!
RE ROO!
EMPLOYEES ONLY
LOOK! THERE'S WATER COMING FROM UNDER THIS DOOR!
LET'S CHECK IT OUT!
JINKIES! WHY IS IT SO DARK IN HERE?
WHAT ARE YOU KIDS DOING?
WE'RE INVESTIGATING THE LAGOON CREATURE!
AND YOU DIDN'T HAVE TO SCARE US LIKE THAT!
MAY WE ASK WHO YOU ARE?
HULETT
I'M THE LANDSCAPER. NAME'S HULETT. I TAKE CARE OF THE GROUNDS!
SO, THIS WATER IN FRONT OF YOUR LOCKER...
I WAS ADJUSTING THE SPRINKLERS.
MUST'VE TRACKED IT IN.

DO YOU KNOW ANYTHING ABOUT MR. ORSON, THE ACTOR?
SURE, I SEEN HIM. BUT IF YOU'RE AUTOGRAPH HUNTERS, FORGET IT! HE'S A LONER AND DOESN'T SEE ANYONE!
KA-CHUK!
SEAWEED? HOW'D THAT GET ON MY BACK? HMM, BETTER SAVE IT. IT MIGHT BE A CLUE!
RAGGY, RUT'S RIS?
BUT MY NOSE HAS A CLUE THAT NEARBY THERE'S...
SNIFF
SNIFF
ROOD!!
YOU SAID IT, SCOOB! I NEVER MET A MEAL I DIDN'T LIKE!

WOULD YOU LIKE TO TRY ONE OF OUR LOCAL DISHES? THIS ONE IS CALLED "POI"!
POI-OH-POI! I'LL TRY ANY FOOD ANY TIME!
RHEE, HEE, HEE, HEE!
MARK THIS DATE ON THE CALENDAR, SCOOB! I FINALLY MET A MEAL I DIDN'T LIKE!
RECHHH!!
LIKE, I'M SORRY I INSULTED YOUR FOOD, BUT THAT'S NO REASON TO RUN AWAY SCREAMING!
EEEEEKKK!!
BUT HE IS! LET'S GET THE HECK OUTTA HERE!
RI'M RUNNING!
ROOOAARRRRR!!
SPLOOP!
LIKE, TAKE THIS, 'CAUSE IT WASN'T HELPING MY MOOD ANY MORE THAN YOU ARE!

NOWHERE TO GO FROM HERE BUT INTO THE LAGOON, OLD PAL!
ROO ROLD! BRRR!
BLONK!
?
?
RRROOOOAAARRRR!!
CHOMP!
CHOMP!
LIKE, LET'S HEAD BACK TO THE HOTEL, SCOOB!
ARRRRRRRGHHH!

AGAIN? THIS IS GETTING TO BE A BAD HABIT!
LIKE, YOU KNOW HOW HARD HABITS ARE TO KICK!
I WISH ALL THE TOURISTS WOULD GET BANNED FROM THE ISLAND! I'LL BE BACK WHEN YOU'RE GONE!
SHAGGY! SCOOBY! YOU SAW THE CREATURE AGAIN?
WORSE THAN THAT! OL' FISH-FACE SAW US!
WHERE DID YOU PICK UP ALL THIS SEAWEED?
YEAH! YOU'RE BEGINNING TO LOOK LIKE THE CREATURE YOURSELF!
ROVER RERE!
LIKE, THERE MUST BE TEN POUNDS OF IT UNDER THAT DESK!
HMMM... THAT DESK CLERK SURE HATES THE TOURISTS!
AND THIS SEAWEED CAME FROM THE LAGOON!
THE SAND ON IT MATCHES THE TEXTURE AND COLOR FROM THAT SIDE OF THE ISLAND!
WE BETTER FOLLOW HIM TONIGHT AND SEE WHAT HE DOES!
GOOD! WHILE YOU DO THAT, SCOOB AND I WILL CATCH SOME SHUT-EYE!
NOT SO FAST, YOU TWO! WE NEED YOUR EYES OPEN!

THAT NIGHT...
THERE'S THE CLERK! I HAD A HUNCH HE WOULD COME DOWN HERE!
WHY? IS HE THE CREATURE'S FRIEND?
SHAGGY, WE THINK HE IS THE CREATURE!
HOLD IT RIGHT THERE! WE CAUGHT YOU RED-HANDED!
OR SEAWEED-HANDED!
SEE WHAT I MEAN? YOU CAN'T DO ANYTHING ON THIS ISLAND WITHOUT GETTING ACCOSTED BY THE TOURISTS!
YES! AND THAT'S WHY YOU'VE BEEN DRESSING UP AS THE CREATURE TO SCARE ALL THE TOURISTS OFF THE ISLAND!
I'M NOT THE CREATURE!
THEN, LIKE, WHAT'S WITH ALL THE SEAWEED?
I'M STUDYING TO BE A BOTANIST! I'VE BEEN IDENTIFYING ALL THE SEAWEED ON THE ISLAND. I JUST CAN'T STAND ALL THE INTERRUPTIONS DURING TOURIST SEASON!
RUH RO!
BOY, ARE OUR FACES RED! WAIT -- DOES THAT MEAN THE CREATURE IS REAL?
I DOUBT IT, SHAGGY!
BUT WHOEVER IS POSING AS THE CREATURE ISN'T LIVING IN THE LAGOON!
HOW DOES HE GET IN AND OUT WITHOUT ANYONE SEEING HIM?
I'VE SEEN A RUNOFF DRAIN DOWN THERE WHEN I DIVE FOR SEAWEED!
SHORTLY...
WHY DO I HAVE TO GO DOWN THERE?
YOU'RE THE ONLY ONE THIS SCUBA GEAR WOULD FIT!
ARGH! YOU'D THINK WITH ALL I EAT, I'D HAVE BULKED UP BY NOW!

LIKE, SO LONG, SCOOB, OLD BUDDY! IT'S BEEN NICE KNOWING YOU!
RYE, RAGGY! ROO HOO HOO!
HERE'S A SCOOBY SNACK FOR OLD TIMES' SAKE!
STOP BEING SO DRAMATIC! YOU'RE COMING BACK!
YEAH? TELL THAT TO THE CREATURE!
RHERE'D RAT RACK RAND?
!
ROOOOAAARRRR!!
RELP! RAGGY!

RUN, SCOOBY DOO!
YOU'LL MAKE ONE HECK OF A SUSHI MEAL, YOU EVIL CREATURE!
CLARNG!
LIKE, OW! MY NOGGIN!
NOW TO SEE WHO'S BEHIND THIS CREATURE FEATURE!
GOTCHA, MR. CREATURE!
YEAH! HEE, HEE, OW!
GOOD WORK LEADING HIM INTO THE NET, SCOOBY!
MR. HULETT, THE LANDSCAPER!
SO THOSE PUDDLES OF WATER WERE FROM THE COSTUME -- HIDDEN IN YOUR LOCKER!
BUT WHY? THE ONLY OTHER PERSON WHO HAD A MOTIVE WAS MAURICE ORSON, THE ISLAND'S NEW OWNER!
AND YOU WERE RIGHT -- I'M WORKING FOR HIM!
HE KEPT TRYING TO BUY THE HOTEL AND SHUT IT DOWN. WHEN MR. HA WOULDN'T SELL, HE HIRED ME TO SCARE EVERYONE OFF THE ISLAND SO THE HOTEL WOULD CLOSE!

LATER...
I WOULD'VE HAD THE ISLAND TO MYSELF IF IT WASN'T FOR THOSE MEDDLING KIDS! I'M SELLING THE ISLAND AND MOVING BACK TO BEVERLY HILLS! I GET MORE PEACE IN THE CITY!
POLICE
I GUESS THAT ABOUT WRAPS IT UP!
NOT QUITE! SCOOB AND I STILL HAVE SOME UNFINISHED BUSINESS!
SUGAR!
RUGAR!
SYRUP!
RYRUP!
WHIPPED CREAM!
REAM!
CHERRIES!
RERRIES!
NOW THAT'S GOOD POI!
LIKE, MY RECORD STANDS! I STILL HAVEN'T MET A MEAL I DIDN'T LIKE!
ROOBY ROOBY ROO!!
THE END

WELCOME TO ROSWELL, GANG! THE SITE OF THE MOST FAMOUS "TRUE" U.F.O. INCIDENTS OF ALL TIME!
YOU MEAN THE UFOS BLEW UP THE WHITE HOUSE HERE? LIKE, I THOUGHT THE WHITE HOUSE WAS IN WASHINGTON D.C.?!
THAT WAS JUST A MOVIE, SILLY!
AHHHHHH!!!! VELMA, LOOK OUT!
LIKE, THERE'S AN ALIEN RIGHT NOW!!!
WELCOME TO ROSWELL NEW M
RELAX, SHAGGY! IT'S ONLY A SIGN. SEE?
YEAH, LIKE ONLY A SIGN WE'VE BEEN INVADED BY OUTER SPACE GUYS!
THE MYSTERY MACHINE
WELCOME TO ROSWELL NEW MEXICO
ONE NIGHT in ROSWELL Part One:
SPIES from the SKIES!
writer: AURIK TYLER pencils: JOE STATON
inks: ANDREW PEPOY letters: JOHN COSTANZA
colors: PAUL BECTON assists: HARVEY RICHARDS
edits: DANA KURTIN

WELL, THEY DO SAY THAT BACK IN 1947, A COUPLE OF FLYING SAUCERS CRASHED HERE IN ROSWELL-- AND THAT THE ARMY HID THOSE SHIPS AT A NEARBY ARMY AIRFIELD HANGAR!
AND THERE'S THE STORY ABOUT THE ROSWELL RANCHER WHO FOUND STRANGE ALIEN SILVER WRECKAGE OUT IN THE MIDDLE OF NOWHERE!
AND THE ONE ABOUT THE JET PILOT WHO SAID HE SAW A FORMATION OF NINE FLYING "DISKS" MOVING AT OVER 1,200 MILES PER HOUR OVER THE ROSWELL DESERT!
DON'T FORGET THE GUY WHO SAW ONE ALIEN GIVING FIRST AID TO THE OTHER ALIEN CRASH VICTIMS!
WHAT ABOUT HOW THE ARMY ACTUALLY PUT OUT A PRESS RELEASE SAYING THAT THEY HAD A FLYING SAUCER IN THEIR POSSESSION!
WINK!
RIPES!!!
RET'S RET ROUTTA RERE!
WOW! I'VE NEVER SEEN SCOOBY SO ANXIOUS TO GET ON A CASE!
I HAVE -- BUT THEN IT WAS A "CASE" OF SCOOBY SNACKS! GET IT??
ROSV
NEW MEX

SCOOB'S JUST BEING SMART. LIKE, HE DOESN'T WANT ANYTHING TO DO WITH ANY ALIENS.
WELL, DON'T WORRY, WE'RE NOT HERE ABOUT ALIENS.
RHEW!
WE'RE HERE ABOUT FLYING SAUCERS!
WHAT!!??
ROHHHH!
SPECIFICALLY, WE'RE HERE TO HELP A SCIENTIST NAMED DR. GOOLUNK.
HE SENT AN E-MAIL TO OUR WEB PAGE SAYING THAT SOMEONE WAS OUT TO STEAL HIS TOP-SECRET EXPERIMENTAL FLYING SAUCER PLANS!
FIGURES A MAD SCIENTIST LIVES HERE--
--EVEN HIS HOUSE LOOKS LIKE A FLYING SAUCER!
IT'S CALLED ADOBE. IT'S MADE OF SUN-DRIED CLAY!
HI! ARE YOU DR. GOOLUNK? WE'RE MYSTERY INC.
YAH YAH HELLO--I'M DOC GOOLUNK!
COME IN! ONLY YOU CAN HELP ME SOLVE THIS MYSTERY!

FOR YEARS I HAVE BEEN WORKING ON AMAZING ALTERNATIVE FORMS OF PROPULSION. YOU CAN SEE ALL MY DESIGNS THROUGHOUT MY HOUSE, YAH?
AND NOW SOMEONE IS SNEAKING INTO MY HOME AND STEALING THE PLANS FOR MY SPACESHIP!
HEY SCOOB, LIKE, IF THIS IS A DISH, IT WOULD LOOK BETTER WITH SOME SPAGHETTI IN IT!
RAGHETTI... RUMMY!
I WAS ASLEEP IN THE LAB WHEN THEY STRUCK THE FIRST TIME! I SCARED THEM OFF, BUT I KNOW THEY WILL BE BACK, BECAUSE THEY MISSED THE MOST IMPORTANT ENGINE BLUEPRINTS--
SPAGHETTI, ICE CREAM, CHOCOLATE LAYER CAKE...
HEY! PLEASE, NOT TO TOUCH MY TEST MODEL!!
VRMMMMM
YIKES! LOOK OUT!
WOW, DOC! THAT BABY REALLY MOVES!
YAH! THE BABY MOVES GOOD!
ZZZZZZZOOM!
BUT NOW WE PUT MY BABY TO BED, YAH?
SORRY, PROFESSOR! LIKE, I'M A MYSTERY-SOLVER, NOT A BABY-SITTER!
AND NOW I'LL, LIKE, HELP SOLVE THE MYSTERY OF HOW TO PICK UP THIS MESS I MADE!
CLIK!

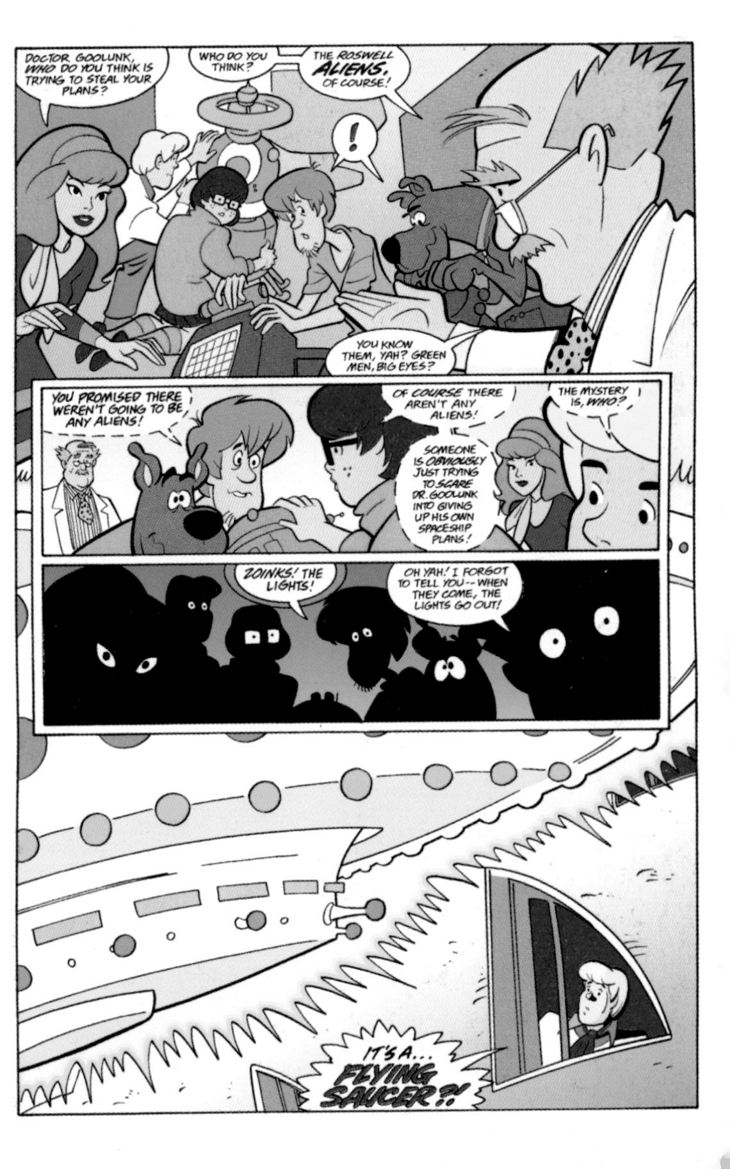
DOCTOR GOOLUNK, WHO DO YOU THINK IS TRYING TO STEAL YOUR PLANS?
WHO DO YOU THINK?
THE ROSWELL ALIENS, OF COURSE!
!
YOU KNOW THEM, YAH? GREEN MEN, BIG EYES?
YOU PROMISED THERE WEREN'T GOING TO BE ANY ALIENS!
OF COURSE THERE AREN'T ANY ALIENS!
SOMEONE IS OBVIOUSLY JUST TRYING TO SCARE DR. GOOLUNK INTO GIVING UP HIS OWN SPACESHIP PLANS!
THE MYSTERY IS, WHO?
ZOINKS! THE LIGHTS!
OH YAH! I FORGOT TO TELL YOU -- WHEN THEY COME, THE LIGHTS GO OUT!
IT'S A... FLYING SAUCER?!

WE NEED A PLAN-- WHAT SHOULD WE DO?
HIDE!!
HERE! I HAVE JUST WHAT WE NEED!
GREAT! DOC. GOOLUNK'S GOT A BUILT-IN HIDING PLACE!
WAIT, SHAGGY! DON'T TOUCH THAT...
KKRATCHA-WONK
...SWITCH.
HEY DOC. LIKE, I DON'T WANT TO COM-PLAIN, BUT THIS IS AN EVEN WORSE HIDING PLACE THAN UNDER THE COUCH!
THAT IS MAYBE BECAUSE THAT IS NOT A HIDING PLACE! IT IS SUPPOSED TO BE A TRAP FOR THE--
...ALIENS!

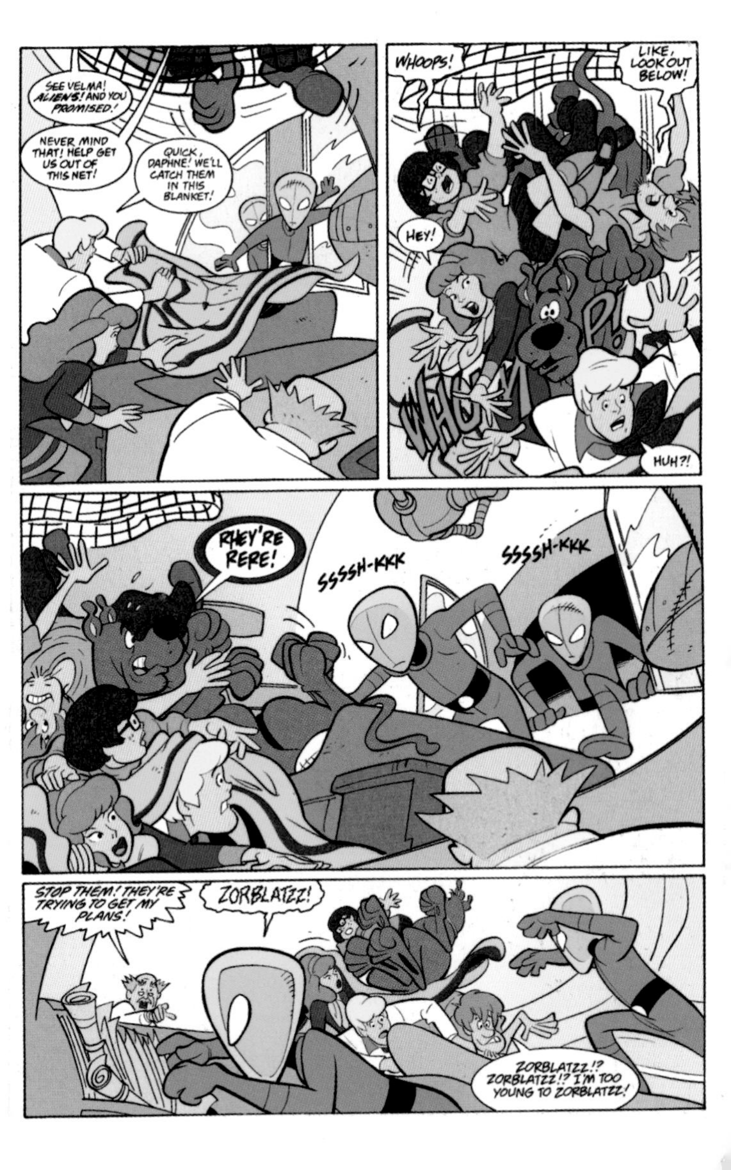
SEE VELMA! ALIENS! AND YOU PROMISED!
NEVER MIND THAT! HELP GET US OUT OF THIS NET!
QUICK, DAPHNE! WE'LL CATCH THEM IN THIS BLANKET!
WHOOPS!
LIKE, LOOK OUT BELOW!
HEY!
WHUMP!
HUH?!
RHEY'RE RERE!
SSSSH-KKK
SSSSH-KKK
STOP THEM! THEY'RE TRYING TO GET MY PLANS!
ZORBLATZZ!
ZORBLATZZ!? ZORBLATZZ!? I'M TOO YOUNG TO ZORBLATZZ!

YOU LITTLE MEN STOP GOING THROUGH MY THINGS THIS INSTANT! I--
RUN, SCOOB, THEY'RE GAINING ON US!
CRASSSHH
OOOF! WHO IS CRAZIER, THE ALIENS OR YOU BOYS?!
LIKE, DEJA VU! SORRY, DOC!
I FEEL LIKE A PINBALL, YAH? OOP!
BONG
POKK
LIKE WOW, DOC! YOUR NOSE CALLED UP THE PERFECT ALIEN WEAPON--A RAY GUN!
SPOING!
I'LL HAVE THIS WORKING IN A JIFFY! C'MON, SCOOB!
PRAZZA ZIL NIK NIK!
GOSH, THAT DOESN'T LOOK LIKE A RAY GUN, SHAG! IT LOOKS LIKE A--

SPOOSH!
--EMERGENCY FIRE HOSE!
OH, WELL, THIS IS AN EMERGENCY!
BUT SHAGGY--
--THE WATER IS MELTING DR. GOOLUNK'S MUD WALLS!!
SPOOSH!
QUICK, SCOOB! TURN IT OFF!
RHY'M RYING!
OKAY, GREEN GUY! I'VE GOT YOU N--
OOOFFFF!
SPOOSH!
SHAGGY!
PRAZZA ZIL BOINGALONG!
WHOA!
SHAGGY!
SPOOSH!
SLIPPP
SPOOSH!
LIKE, WHY IS THIS ALL MY FAULT?!
BECAUSE YOU'RE THE ONE WITH THE HOSE!

THEY'VE GOT THE PLANS! QUICK, SHAGGY--
ZURGLE BLOTZ!
--BLAST 'EM!
BULL'S-EYE!
SPLOOSH!
BLOOSH!!
GREAT AIM, SHAGGY! YOUR WATER HOSE CAUGHT THE ALIENS IN THE MUDSLIDE!
THEY'RE STUCK FAST!
OH, JUST LUCKY, I GUESS...
RUCKY? RUD? RUCK!
COME ON, LET'S SEE WHO THESE GUYS ARE!

MY GOODNESS! THEY ARE NOT ALIENS AT ALL!
DOCTOR GOOLUNK, DO YOU KNOW EITHER OF THESE MEN?
NOPE! SEE, SHAGGY? THEY'RE JUST PEOPLE IN LITTLE GREEN SUITS TRYING TO SCARE THE PROFESSOR AND STEAL HIS PLANS!
I KNOW THAT I DO NOT KNOW THEM. THESE ARE STRANGE STRANGERS TO ME!
WELL, SINCE YOU'RE DOING SUCH TOP-SECRET EXPERIMENTS, I HAVE A HUNCH--
SLAM!
PARDON US. WE BELIEVE TWO SUSPECTS HAVE ENTERED YOUR HOUSE.
WOW.
I DON'T BELIEVE IT! REAL LIVE AGENTS IN BLACK!!!
THE MYSTERY MEN WHO ALWAYS SHOW UP TO CLEAN UP AFTER ALIEN EVENTS!
I THOUGHT THEY WERE JUST AN URBAN LEGEND!
YOU KIDS APPREHENDED THE SUSPECTS ON YOUR OWN?! OUTSTANDING!
WE'VE BEEN AFTER THIS BUNCH FOR A WHILE NOW. THEY'VE BEEN POSING AS ALIENS IN ORDER TO COMMIT ROBBERIES ALL OVER NEW MEXICO, TAKING ADVANTAGE OF ALL OF THOSE SILLY STORIES ABOUT ROSWELL.
LIKE, DID THEY HEAR ABOUT THE ONES WHO BLEW UP THE WHITE HOUSE?
SHHH!

THANK YOU. YOU CITIZENS HAVE MADE OUR JOB MUCH EASIER.
PLEASE FILL OUT THIS REPORT AND SEND IT TO THE ADDRESS LISTED ABOVE. YOU WILL BE CONTACTED.
THIS TURNED OUT TO BE OUR COOLEST CASE EVER!!
MAN! LIKE THE AGENTS IN BLACK ADMITTED THEY COULDN'T SOLVE A CASE WITHOUT US!
WELL, WE HAVE BEEN SOLVING MYSTERIES FOR SOME TIME NOW!
I DON'T BELIEVE IT!!
WHAT THE MATTER, DOCTOR GOOLUNK?
MY PLANS HAVE BEEN STOLEN--
--THOSE AGENTS IN BLACK WERE FAKES!
WILL DOCTOR GOOLUNK RECOVER HIS LIFE'S WORK?
GULP... I'M GETTING A BAD FEELING THIS CASE ISN'T OVER!
CAN MYSTERY INC. GET TO THE BOTTOM OF THIS CREEPY CASE?
FIND OUT--IN THE NEXT INSTALLMENT OF ONE NIGHT IN ROSWELL!

THE MYSTERY INC. GANG HAS COME TO ROSWELL, NEW MEXICO, TO HELP SCIENTIST DR. GOOLUNK SOLVE THE MYSTERY OF THE ALIENS TRYING TO STEAL HIS SECRET SPACESHIP PLANS!
BUT NOW THE MYSTERY IS EVEN BIGGER THAN BEFORE--THE INFAMOUS AGENTS IN BLACK, WHO ALWAYS APPEAR AFTER ALIEN ENCOUNTERS, HAVE STOLEN DR. GOOLUNK'S PLANS THEMSELVES!
CAN THE GANG SOLVE THE MYSTERY AND SAVE DR. GOOLUNK'S WORK? FIND OUT IN...
ONE NIGHT IN ROSWELL Part 2: ATTACK of the AGENTS IN BLACK
writer: RURIK TYLER
pencils: JOE STATON
inks: ANDREW PEPOY
letters: JOHN COSTANZA
colors: PAUL BECTON
assists: HARVEY RICHARDS
edits: DANA KURTIN

IN THE ROSWELL DESERT OUTSIDE OF DR. GOOLUNK'S HOME...
THESE TIRE RACKS HEADING AWAY FROM DOC GOOLUNK'S HOUSE ARE HUGE! DO YOU THINK IT'S A MONSTER TRUCK?
RONSTER RUCK?!
A MONSTER TRUCK!!??! FIRST ALIENS, NOW MONSTERS?!
NO, SHAGGY, NOT A MONSTER, I PROMISE-- A SPECIAL KIND OF TRUCK WITH BIG TIRES.
LOOK AT THIS! SOMEBODY GOT OUT OF THE TRUCK BEFORE IT STARTED DRIVING ON THIS PAVED ROAD. THE FOOTPRINTS HEAD OVER TOWARDS THOSE HILLS!
CHECK OUT THOSE WEIRD LIGHTS!
LIKE, THIS IS A CLOSE ENCOUNTER OF THE SPOOKY KIND!
SHAG, SCOOB AND I'LL FOLLOW THE FOOTPRINTS. YOU TWO TAKE THE PAVED ROAD.
WE'LL MEET YOU ON THE OTHER SIDE OF THE HILL!
HOOOOOOOOOOWL!
RELAX, GUYS. IT'S JUST A COYOTE HOWLING AT THE MOON.
SURE IT'S NOT HOWLING AT CREATURES FROM THE MOON?
OH MAN!
IT'S INCREDIBLE!

--IT'S SOME KIND OF CARNIVAL FOR UFO FANS!
UFO
LIKE, LET'S GET DOWN THERE RIGHT NOW!
YOU THINK THE GIRLS NEED OUR HELP?
NO--I THINK WHERE THERE'S A CARNIVAL, THERE'S JUNK FOOD! WE DON'T HAVE A MOMENT TO LOSE!!
MEANWHILE...
STRANGE! THIS IS THE ANNUAL ROSWELL SCIENCE FACT, FICTION, AND FANTASY CONVENTION! WHY WOULD THE THIEVES COME HERE?
IT'S MYSTERY INC.! PLEASE HELP US!
PARKING
I CAN'T BELIEVE OUR LUCK! WE'VE VISITED YOUR WEBSITE A HUNDRED TIMES! CAN YOU HELP US? SOMEONE'S STOLEN OUR F.M.D.R.s!
SURE! WE'RE ALREADY ON ONE CASE, BUT THE MORE THE MERRIER! ...WHAT'S AN "F.M.D.R."?
CHARTER
IT STANDS FOR FULL MOBILITY DISPLAY ROBOTS. WE HAD TWO OF THEM ON DISPLAY, AND NOW THEY'RE GONE!
THEY LOOK JUST LIKE THIS MODEL, EXCEPT THEY'RE SEVEN FEET TALL AND THEY REALLY WORK!
I DON'T KNOW HOW ANYONE COULD HIDE THEM, BUT THEY'RE GONE!

SOON...
...SO I'M WONDERING IF IT'S ALL CONNECTED! FIRST DR. GOOLUNK'S SPACESHIP PLANS ARE SNATCHED, AND NOW THESE F.M.D.R.S!
WELL, THE GENUINE AGENTS IN BLACK WILL BE HARD TO FIND IN THIS CROWD! EVERYONE HERE IS AN AGENT OR PRETENDING TO BE!
BUT OUR GUYS WALKED RIGHT INTO ALL THE MUD SHAGGY CAUSED WHEN HE USED THE FIRE HOUSE IN DR. GOOLUNK'S ADOBE MANSION.
SO WE'LL JUST LOOK FOR THE AGENTS WITH RED MUD ON THEIR PANTS!
HA HA! LOOKS LIKE SCOOBY FOUND A BIG JELLYFISH.
KNOWING SCOOB, HE THOUGHT IT WAS A PEANUT-BUTTER-AND-JELLYISH!
IT TOOK ME AN HOUR TO GLUE THOSE ON! QUIT IT!
RUM RUM!
HEY! THERE THEY ARE!!
!
AFTER 'EM!
NO PROBLEM!
I--GULP!--DON'T SEE ANY ZIPPERS ON THOSE 'COSTUMES'!
NOW THAT'S A PROBLEM!
GRRRR!

MONSTERS!!!
YOU PROMISED THERE WEREN'T ANY MONSTERS!
ALL RIGHT THEN, ALIENS!!!
YOU PROMISED ME THERE WEREN'T ANY ALIENS! WHY-OH-WHY CAN'T ANYONE KEEP THEIR WORD TO ME?!
HUH? SCOOBY! WHAT'S GOING ON?
RERICIOUS ROUGHRUTS ROM ROUTER RACE!
YOUR DOG IS EATING MY COSTUME!
LOOK OUT!
HEY!
RARR?
HEY YOU'RE RIGHT, SCOOBY, THEY ARE DELI-CIOUS!
SCREEECH!
SHAG AND SCOOB ARE TOO BUSY EATING TO RUN! THERE'S A FIRST... NOT!
DAPHNE, LOOK AT THIS!
THE ALIEN LOOKS LIKE A LIVING CREATURE, BUT ITS SKID MARKS ARE METALLIC!
LET'S GO FIND THOSE TWO INVENTORS AND SEE IF THIS HAS ANYTHING TO DO WITH THEIR STOLEN ROBOTS!
SPEAKING OF INVENTORS, VELMA -- WHY DID DR. GOOLUNK HAVE A HIGH-PRESSURE WATER HOSE IN HIS ADOBE BRICK LIVING ROOM?
GOOD QUESTION! I'LL HAVE TO GIVE THAT SOME THOUGHT!
NICAP

HI, GUYS! DID YOU FIND OUR ROBOTS?
"HOVERCRAFT" SCOOTERS
MAYBE! HAVE YOU GOT ANY KIND OF REMOTE CONTROLLER FOR THEM?
NO, WHOEVER TOOK THE ROBOTS TOOK THEIR CONTROLS, TOO. EXCEPT FOR OUR AUTOMATIC POWER CUT OFF. WE'D JUST NEED TO GET CLOSE.
GREAT! GRAB A HOVERCRAFT-- WE'VE GOT SOME MONSTERS TO SHUT DOWN!
HOVERCRAFT? THIS IS JUST A GO-CART!
GOOD THING, TOO! I DON'T HAVE A PILOT'S LICENSE!
VROOOOM!
SKKRAAKZZZ
IT WORKED! THOSE WERE OUR ROBOTS, ALL RIGHT!
BUT WHY ARE THEY HIDDEN UNDER THOSE WACKY SUITS? I MEAN, NO ONE COULD BELIEVE THOSE WERE REAL ALIENS!
OH, UH... ;ahem!; GOT ME!
Whew, OUR F.M.D.R.s BACK AGAIN, SAFE AND SOUND!
THEIR SUITS WERE MADE OF FLEXIBLE MOLDED RUBBER, VELMA! THAT'S WHY WE DIDN'T SEE A ZIPPER OR A SEAM!
BUT WHO WAS CONTROLLING THEM AND CHASING US -- AND WHY?

WELL, WE KNOW IT WASN'T OUR INVENTOR FRIENDS. SOMEONE STOLE THOSE ROBOTS AND THEIR REMOTES.
I BET WE'LL GET OUR ANSWERS WHEN WE FIND OUR AGENTS IN BLACK. BUT WE'VE LOST THEIR TRAIL BY NOW. WHERE DO WE START?
NO WE HAVEN'T--
SECOND CRASH SITE
--THERE THEY ARE NOW!
REE HEE HEE! RHY'LL RHET RHEM RITH RHIS RAUGER RIDE!
SCOOBY! BE CAREFUL!
ROOPS. RISSED!
SWOOSH!
HEY! MY FACE!
PAF!
RUH?
RHUT'S RHIS?

OH, SCOOBY! ARE YOU ALL RIGHT?
LIKE, NICE TRY, BUDDY! HEY, WHAT'S THAT GREASY STUFF ON YOUR PAW?
RICKY RUFFY!
IT'S MAKE-UP!
C'MON, THE AGENTS HIT A DEAD END! WE'VE GOT THEM NOW!
ARTIFACTS FROM THE 509th CENTURY THE GOVERNMENT WANTS TO KEEP THEM FROM YOU-- Take A Pamphlet! Learn More!
JET PACKS
LIKE, THEY'RE PUTTING ON THE JETPACKS!
HURRY! GRAB THEM BEFORE THEY TAKE OFF!
OOOF! THEY'RE GOING TOO FAST!
SPOOOSH!
I...I DON'T BELIEVE IT! THEY WERE WEARING MASKS, TOO!
THE AGENTS IN BLACK ARE--
ALIENS!

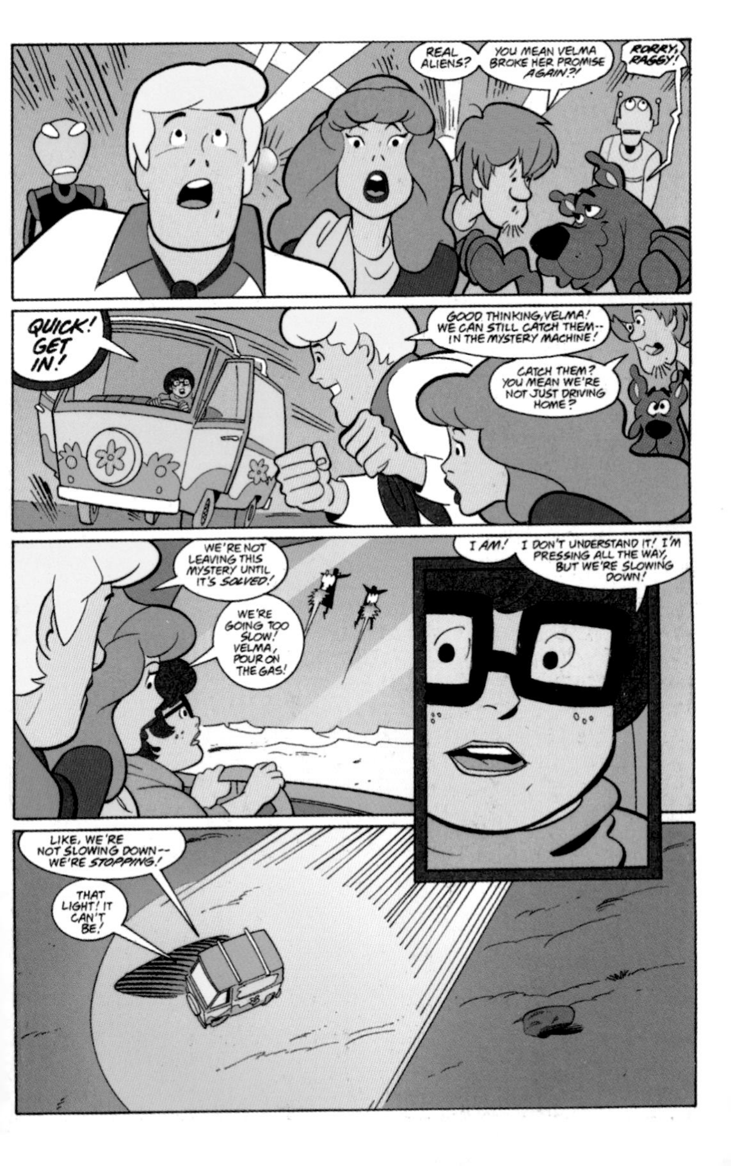
REAL ALIENS?
YOU MEAN VELMA BROKE HER PROMISE AGAIN?!
RORRY, RAGGY!
QUICK! GET IN!
GOOD THINKING, VELMA! WE CAN STILL CATCH THEM-- IN THE MYSTERY MACHINE!
CATCH THEM? YOU MEAN WE'RE NOT JUST DRIVING HOME?
WE'RE NOT LEAVING THIS MYSTERY UNTIL IT'S SOLVED!
WE'RE GOING TOO SLOW! VELMA, POUR ON THE GAS!
I AM!
I DON'T UNDERSTAND IT! I'M PRESSING ALL THE WAY, BUT WE'RE SLOWING DOWN!
LIKE, WE'RE NOT SLOWING DOWN-- WE'RE STOPPING!
THAT LIGHT! IT CAN'T BE!

IT...IT'S A FLYING SAUCER--
--AND IT'S PULLING US UP!
THE MYSTERY MACHINE
REEEEEEEEEELP!
HAS MYSTERY INC. FINALLY MET THEIR MATCH? IS THIS THE ONE MYSTERY THEY CANNOT SOLVE?!
JOIN US NEXT ISSUE FOR THE EXCITING CONCLUSION TO ONE NIGHT IN ROSWELL: FLYING SAUCER FACE-OFF!

THE STORY SO FAR: MYSTERY INC. IS IN ROSWELL, NEW MEXICO, WORLD-FAMOUS SITE OF U.F.O. ENCOUNTERS--
WELCOME TO ROSWELL NEW MEXICO
--TO HELP PROFESSOR GOOLUNK SAVE HIS FLYING SAUCER PLANS FROM THIEVING ALIENS!
THE GANG SOLVES THE MYSTERY AND UNMASKS THE ALIENS--
--WHEN THE FABLED AGENTS IN BLACK ARRIVE TO WRAP UP THE CASE!
BUT THEN THE AGENTS STEAL PROFESSOR GOOLUNK'S PLANS THEMSELVES--
--AND USE STOLEN EXPERIMENTAL ROBOTS TO FOIL THE GANG AT A LOCAL UFO CONVENTION!
UFO
FINALLY THE GANG CATCHES UP, ONLY TO DISCOVER THE AGENTS ARE ALIENS THEMSELVES!
AND NOW THE GANG HAS BEEN... ABDUCTED BY A U.F.O.?!
THE MYSTERY MACHINE

IS THIS THE END OF MYSTERY INC.? FIND OUT IN--
ONE NIGHT IN ROSWELL
Part 3:
FLYING SAUCER FACE-OFF!
WRITER: RURIK TYLER
PENCILS: JOE STATON
INKS: ANDREW PEPOY
LETTERS: JOHN COSTANZA
COLORS: PAUL BECTON
ASSISTS: HARVEY RICHARDS
EDITS: DANA KURTIN
HEIDI MacDONALD
UNBELIEVABLE! THAT'S A REAL U.F.O.!!!
THEY'RE COMING FOR US, FRED! HEAR THAT HORRIBLE CLACKING SOUND?
CLACK CLACK CLACK
TH-TH-THAT'S NOT A U.F.O., DAPHNE--THAT'S MY TEETH CHATTERING!
HALLO, KIDS! HALLO, SCOOBY!
DOC GOOLUNK?!?
YAH! IT'S ME!
NOW YOU KNOW THE REASON THOSE FAKE ALIENS WANTED MY FLYING SAUCER PLANS--THEY WORKED!
THE MYSTERY MACHINE

LET ME GUESS-- YOU HID THIS HUGE SHIP UNDER YOUR ADOBE MUD HOUSE, RIGHT?
AND THAT'S WHY YOU HAD A HIGH-PRESSURE HOSE IN YOUR FLOOR-- TO MELT THE WALLS SO YOU COULD GET YOUR SAUCER OUT! *
YAH, YOU ARE RIGHT, VELMA! I KNEW I HAD TO COME HELP YOU KIDS!
* See SCOOBY-DOO #26, Part I! -D.K.
SO, FREDDY, DID YOU KIDS GET MY FLYING SAUCER PLANS FROM THOSE AGENTS IN BLACK?
SUCH A RELIEF THAT ALIENS DID NOT REALLY STEAL THEM!
I'M SORRY, DOC GOOLUNK...
...BUT ALIENS DID STEAL YOUR PLANS! THE AGENTS WERE WEARING HUMAN MASKS!
OH NO!
AND, LIKE, I DON'T KNOW HOW TO TELL YOU THIS, BUT--
--THERE'S ONE NOW!!!
IT LOOKS LIKE HE'S HEADING TOWARD THAT MILITARY BASE!
QUICK, DOC, LOWER DOWN THE MYSTERY MACHINE AND WE'LL CHASE HIM ON FOOT!

COULD THIS BE THE ROSWELL ARMY BASE OF ALL THOSE URBAN LEGENDS ABOUT U.F.O.'S?
MAYBE. BUT IT'S NOT EXACTLY LIKE I PICTURED IT!
I'LL HOVER OUT HERE FOR YOU IF YOU NEED ME, YAH?
FREDDY, DOES THE TERM "HANGAR 84" MEAN ANYTHING TO YOU?
SURE! ACCORDING TO UFO LORE, HANGAR 84 IS WHERE THE ARMY STORES THE MYSTERIOUS SILVER WRECKASE FOUND BY A RANCHER OUT IN THE DESERT.
FREDDY, LIKE, DOES THE TERM "LET'S GET OUT OF HERE!" MEAN ANYTHING TO YOU?
HANGER 84
SHAGGY, WHAT ARE YOU AND SCOOBY WEARING?!
OUR ANTI-ALIEN SUITS!
I THOUGHT THOSE WERE YOUR ANTI-BIGFOOT SUITS.
THAT WAS THEN, THIS IS NOW!
EWW! THIS ICKY RUBBER-CEMENTY STUFF IS EVERYWHERE! I WONDER WHAT IT'S FOR?
HEY, LOOK! THE COBWEBS ON THIS DOOR HAVE BEEN RECENTLY BROKEN. SO SOMEONE'S BEEN THROUGH HERE RECENTLY! BUT WHO?
VRRRRMMMMM!!
LIKE, I THINK WE'RE ABOUT TO FIND OUT!!!

THERE'S AN ALIEN DRIVING THAT TANK!
AND I BET HE DOESN'T EVEN HAVE A LICENSE!
RIPES!
QUICK, EVERYONE INTO THE HANGAR!!
VRRMMMM
LIKE, WHAT'S ALL THIS STUFF?
REAH! RESSY!
I KNOW ONE THING-- DOC GOOLUNK'S PLANS ARE IN THAT BRIEF-CASE!
KRASSHH!
HEY! THIS GUY DOESN'T TAKE "NO" FOR AN ANSWER!
TRY SAYING IT IN ALIEN-ESE!
TRY SAYING IT LATER! I'VE GOT THE CASE!
WHOOOOSH!
HEY! GIVE THAT BACK!

HEY, LIKE, LOOK WHAT I FOUND, SCOOB! I DIDN'T KNOW ALIENS LIKED SNACKS!
RALIEN RACKS? ROOL!
SAUCER SNACKS
WOOOOOSSHH
HEY, I DIDN'T KNOW DAPHNE COULD FLY EITHER!
ROCKET RACKS? REARRY ROOL!
NAB!
THANK YOOOOU VERY MUCH!
HERE SCOOBY! CATCH!
HEAD FOR DOC GOOLUNK'S SHIP, SCOOB!
ROT RIT!
RHO RHO! RHIT'S ROT REE!
ROC ROORUNK! REEEEELP!
VEEEOOOOO

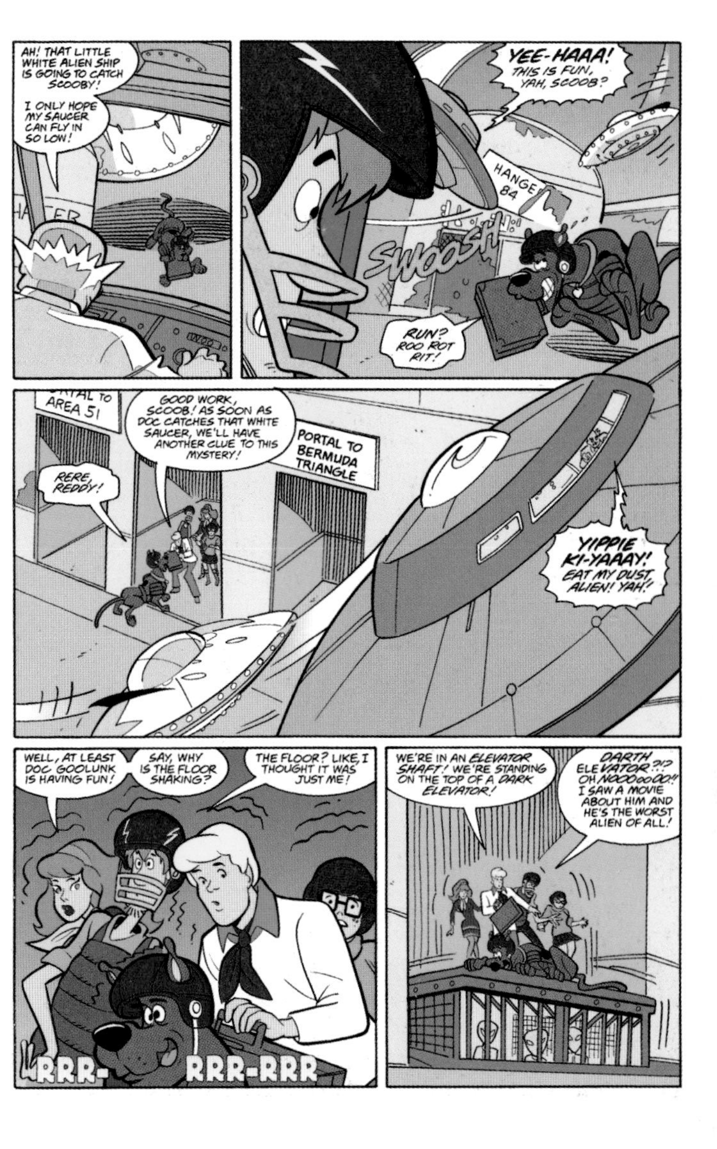
AH! THAT LITTLE WHITE ALIEN SHIP IS GOING TO CATCH SCOOBY!
I ONLY HOPE MY SAUCER CAN FLY IN SO LOW!
YEE-HAAA! THIS IS FUN, YAH, SCOOB?
HANGER 84
SWOOSH
RUN? ROO ROT RIT!
AREA 51
GOOD WORK, SCOOB! AS SOON AS DOC CATCHES THAT WHITE SAUCER, WE'LL HAVE ANOTHER CLUE TO THIS MYSTERY!
PORTAL TO BERMUDA TRIANGLE
RERE, REDDY!
YIPPIE KI-YAAAY! EAT MY DUST, ALIEN! YAH!
WELL, AT LEAST DOC GOOLUNK IS HAVING FUN!
SAY, WHY IS THE FLOOR SHAKING?
THE FLOOR? LIKE, I THOUGHT IT WAS JUST ME!
RRR- RRR-RRR
WE'RE IN AN ELEVATOR SHAFT! WE'RE STANDING ON THE TOP OF A DARK ELEVATOR!
DARTH ELEVATOR?!? OH NOOOooOO!! I SAW A MOVIE ABOUT HIM AND HE'S THE WORST ALIEN OF ALL!

JUMP!
THAT WAS CLOSE! WE WERE ALMOST PANCAKES!
PANCAKES? LIKE, THEY DON'T WANT TO EAT US, DO THEY?!
NO--IT LOOKS LIKE THEY JUST WANT THE BRIEFCASE!
YOU KNOW, FOR ALIENS THEY ACT MORE LIKE PURSE SNATCH-ERS!
GULP... DON'T WE GET ONE LAST SCOOBY SNACK?
HEY GANG! IT'S DOC GOOLUNK!
RUN? RUST RUN?! RAWWW!
STRANGE THAT SAUCER DOES NOT FOLLOW ME UP HERE. IT ONLY HUNTS ME WHEN I AM DOWN LOW!
I WILL SHOW IT WHO IS BOSS! NOW I GO TO SAVE THE KIDS!
HANG ON, KIDS! THIS RESCUE STUFF I'M STILL NEW AT! DUCK!

GAK! AGAIN THE SAUCER COMES TO ME DOWN LOW!
WATCH THE CRAZY DRIVING, WHITE SHIP! YOU WILL MAKE US BOTH CRASH!
VOOOM
GO, DOC GOOLUNK!
THAT WHITE SHIP SURE DOES FLY WEIRD. IT'S LIKE IT'S ON A STRING!
RAGGY! RAGGY, ROOK!
ANOTHER SAUCER? WHAT IS THIS? A USED CAR LOT FOR SPACEMEN?
WSSHHH
THAT LITTLE GREEN SAUCER JUST CUT RIGHT IN FRONT OF THE WHITE ONE!
THE WHITE ONE'S FALLING!
CRASSHHH!
LOOK OUT!

LOOK AT THAT! IT'S A FAKE!
IT'S JUST AN EMPTY SHELL MADE OF PLYWOOD!
LIKE, MAYBE IT HAS SOME IN-FLIGHT SNACKS WE COULD BORROW!
RETZELS? REANUTS?
IT ALL MAKES SENSE! SOMEONE HUNG A MODEL UFO FROM THAT CRANE AND SWUNG IT TO LOOK LIKE A REAL UFO!
THAT CRANE'S GIANT TIRES WOULD ACCOUNT FOR THE HUGE TRACKS WE FOUND BY DOC GOOLUNK'S HOUSE!*
I HAVE A HUNCH OUR AGENTS IN BLACK AND THESE "ALIENS" ARE ALL WORKING TOGETHER! BUT WHY?
*See Scooby #26 part II! --D.K.
HEY! THERE GO OUR SUSPECTS!
DOC GOOLUNK, STOP THAT TRUCK!!!
YIPPIE KII-YAYYY! DOC GOOLUNK WILL LASSO THEM!
VROOM
I WILL DRIVE THEM INTO THE GROUND, YAH?
SCREEE!
KEEP OUT
RESTRICTED

THAT DOC GOOLUNK IS SOME COWBOY!
NOW LET'S GET TO THE BOTTOM OF THIS CASE!
HAH! YOU THINK PARALLEL PARKING IS HARD? TRY PER-PENDICULAR PARKING!
HERE'S ONE CASE, FRED-- THE ONE WITH DOC GOOLUNK'S PLANS AND A WHOLE BUNCH OF OTHER PAPERS!
ALL RIGHT, FELLAS, WHAT'S THE STORY?
WE AIN'T GOT TO TELL YOU NUTHIN'.
NO, BUT YOU DO HAVE TO TELL THE POLICE! GOOD TIMING! WHO CALLED THE SHERIFF?
I DID, FROM MY SAUCER! CELL PHONES ARE AMAZING, YAH?
WHAT'S GOING ON HERE?
ACCORDING TO THESE PAPERS-- THE SCAM OF A LIFETIME!
THESE GUYS WERE BUILDING A A ROSWELL THEME PARK--AND INSTEAD OF BUILDING ROBOTS AND FLYING SAUCERS, THEY DECIDED TO STEAL THEM!
THEY KNEW NO ONE WOULD BELIEVE THAT ALIENS OR AGENTS IN BLACK WERE REALLY THE CULPRITS!
NO ONE, THAT IS--BUT MYSTERY INC.
THAT'S WHY THEY HAD TWO COSTUMES -- ONE AS ALIENS, ONE AS AGENTS IN BLACK! IF ONE SCAM DIDN'T WORK, THE OTHER ONE WOULD!
WEREN'T YOU HOT UNDER THOSE MASKS, BUDDY?
ARE YOU KIDDING? I'M SWEATING A FLOOD IN HERE!

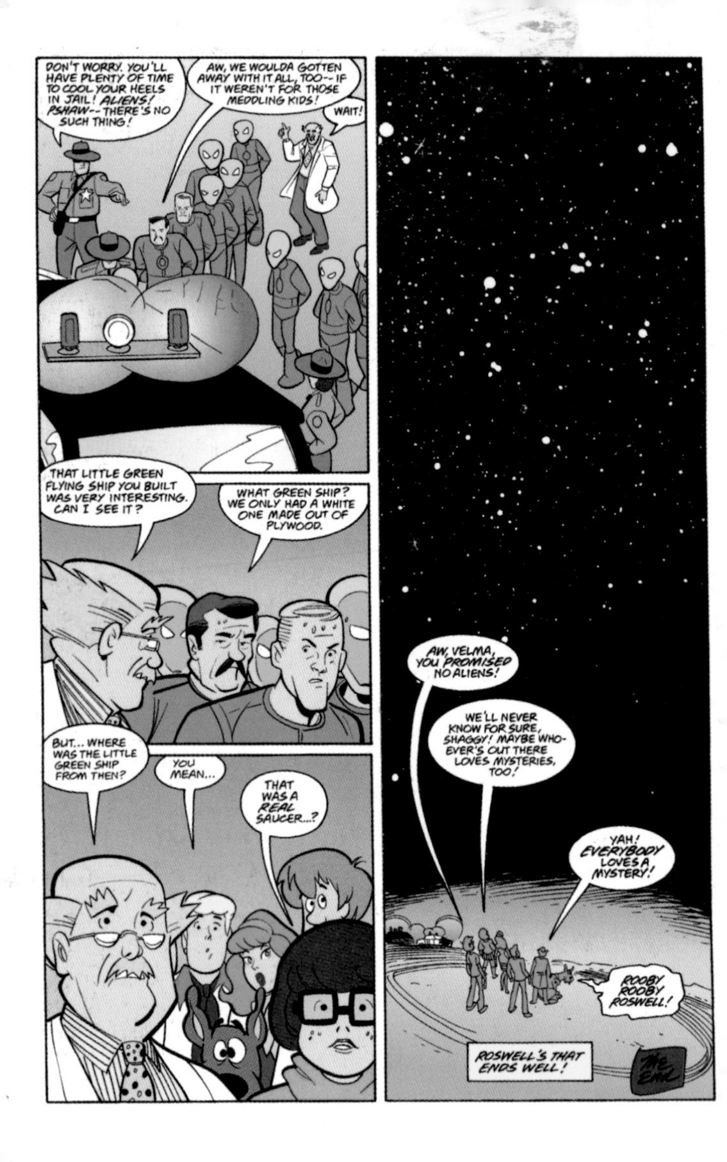
DON'T WORRY. YOU'LL HAVE PLENTY OF TIME TO COOL YOUR HEELS IN JAIL! ALIENS! PSHAW-- THERE'S NO SUCH THING!
AW, WE WOULDA GOTTEN AWAY WITH IT ALL, TOO-- IF IT WEREN'T FOR THOSE MEDDLING KIDS!
WAIT!
THAT LITTLE GREEN FLYING SHIP YOU BUILT WAS VERY INTERESTING. CAN I SEE IT?
WHAT GREEN SHIP? WE ONLY HAD A WHITE ONE MADE OUT OF PLYWOOD.
BUT... WHERE WAS THE LITTLE GREEN SHIP FROM THEN?
YOU MEAN...
THAT WAS A REAL SAUCER...?
AW, VELMA, YOU PROMISED NO ALIENS!
WE'LL NEVER KNOW FOR SURE, SHAGGY! MAYBE WHO-EVER'S OUT THERE LOVES MYSTERIES, TOO!
YAH! EVERYBODY LOVES A MYSTERY!
ROOBY ROOBY ROSWELL!
ROSWELL'S THAT ENDS WELL!
THE END

THE CASE OF THE GREEDY TAR
RUN FOR YOUR LIVES!!! IT'S THE TAR MONSTER!
BRETT LEWIS- WRITER
VINCENT DEPORTER- ARTIST
RYAN CLINE- LETTERER
PAUL BECTON- COLORIST
DIGITAL CHAMELEON- SEPARATIONS
HARVEY RICHARDS- ASST. EDITOR
JOAN HILTY- EDITOR
THE NEXT DAY...
THE MUSEUM BOARD HAS DECIDED NOT TO RISK SCARING AWAY PATRONS BY INVOLVING THE POLICE. THAT'S WHY I CALLED YOU KIDS-- ANY HELP WOULD BE APPRECIATED!
ALSO, DURING EACH RAMPAGE, ANCIENT ARTIFACTS GO MISSING. ALL THAT'S LEFT IN THEIR PLACE ARE GIANT FOOTPRINTS OF TAR...
YIKES!

--FOOTPRINTS THAT LEAD BACK TO THE DEPTHS OF THE HISTORIC TAR PIT ON OUR MUSEUM GROUNDS.
BUT WHAT WOULD SOME CREATURE WANT WITH THOSE ARTIFACTS?
SOUNDS LIKE FOUL PLAY, ALL RIGHT!
FOUL PLAY? HOW DO YOU MEAN?
WELL, THIS TYPE OF MYSTERY OFTEN TURNS OUT TO BE A HOAX THAT COVERS UP A THEFT.
BUT NO ONE EVER PASSED THE GUARDS AT THE GATES!
WHY STEAL ANYTHING IF THEY CAN'T GET IT OFF THE GROUNDS TO SELL IT?
THIS IS OUR CURATOR--HE'S A LITTLE SHOOK UP.
AN ANCIENT EVIL IS RECLAIMING ARTIFACTS TAKEN FROM THE PITS--RETURNING THEM TO HISTORY!
THE COSTS ARE STRANGLING US! MISSING TREASURES, EXTRA SECURITY, AND NOW EXTRA GROUNDSKEEPERS TO CLEAN UP ALL THE TAR MESS!
WELL, KIDS-- CAN YOU HELP?
SURE, WE HAVE WAYS TO DEAL WITH MENACING PHENOMENA LIKE THIS. FOR INSTANCE, WE MIGHT TRY--
--A TRAP!

SOON...
GOT EVERYTHING?
SURE, FREDDY-- NO THANKS TO THOSE TWO!
LIKE, HEY, IT COULD BE A LONG NIGHT--WE'RE GONNA NEED SNACKS, RIGHT?
THE MONSTER DISAPPEARS AFTER EACH RAMPAGE BUT NEVER LEAVES THE GROUNDS.
HE MIGHT GO BACK INTO THE PIT--BUT WE'VE GOT TO CATCH HIM DOING IT.
MUSEUM
DIORAMA
PITS
HERE'S THE MUSEUM AND HERE'S THE TAR PIT, WHICH MEANS THE MONSTER HAS TO GO THROUGH THE AREA BETWEEN THEM.
SO, WE'LL SET OUR TRAP--
--RIGHT THERE!
NOW ALL WE NEED IS SOME CHICKENS FOR BAIT!
LIKE, DON'T LOOK AT US!
RRIGHT! ROOK AWAY! RO RICKENS HERE!

MIDNIGHT...
LIKE, IT JUST FIGURES THERE'D HAVE TO BE A CREEPY FOG TONIGHT!
PIPE DOWN, YOU TWO! IT'S NATURAL FOR FOG TO FORM FROM GROUND WATER...
AGH! LIKE, BRING BACK THE FOG!
LIKE, RUN FOR YOUR LIFE, PAL!
REEPERS!
BURBLE
GURGLE
LIKE, HALP! THERE'S A BIG UGLY TAR GUY RIGHT BEHIND US RUNNING MUCH FASTER THAN YOU'D THINK TAR COULD RUN!
BURBLE
GURGLE
OKAY, DAPHNE! LET GO OF THE ROPE!
RIGHT, FREDDY!

CLUNK
LIKE, THAT GOT HIM, EH SCOOB? MAN, I CAN'T BELIEVE WE WERE EVER AFRAID OF OL' BLACKTOP IN THERE!
REE HEE HEE! REAH-REAH!
GLOOOOOP
LIKE, THE ONLY WAY HE COULD HURT US NOW...
R-R-R-RRAGGYY!!
...WOULD BE IF WE WALKED ON HIM BAREFOOT ON A HOT DAY!
GURGLE
RUN, RAGGYY!!!
YOINKS!

BURBLE
GURGLE
UH, I THOUGHT YOU GUYS WERE WAITING FOR THE MONSTER?
OH, WE'RE DONE WAITING!
AAHH!!
DONE WAITING? WHAT DO YOU...
BURBLE
GURGLE
AAHH!!
LIKE, I TOLD YOU!

I THOUGHT YOU SAID THESE THINGS USUALLY TURN OUT TO BE A *HOAX?*
THAT'S RIGHT!
SO WHY ARE WE RUNNING IF IT'S A HOAX?
YOU NEVER KNOW-- THE ONE TIME YOU *DON'T RUN*, IT COULD BE THE *REAL THING!*
AND IF IT IS A HOAX, THE HOAXER MIGHT BE *DANGEROUS...*
BURBLE
GURGLE
AND BESIDES ALL THAT-- HE'S *REALLY SCARY!!!!*
REALLY-REALLY RARY!!!!

C'MON, GANG!
IS HE STILL BACK THERE?! I DON'T HEAR HIM!
LIKE, HOW 'BOUT WE RUN 'TIL WE HIT MEXICO AND THEN STOP TO CHECK!
IT'S THE CURATOR! ARE YOU OKAY?
HE WENT THATAWAY!
SOON AFTER...
THERE'S NO SIGN OF THE MONSTER--IT'S RETURNED TO THE TAR!
THE ANCIENT SPEARHEAD... IT'S GONE! WE'RE RUINED!
HMM.
WHAT IS--IS THAT A SNORKEL?
IT SURE IS, DAPHNE! AND WHEN WE FIGURE OUT WHY IT'S HERE, WE'LL HAVE OUR FIRST BREAK IN THIS CASE!
IT MIGHT HAVE BEEN PICKED UP BY THE CREATURE IN THE PIT--ALL KINDS OF JUNK TURNS UP IN THERE.
WE'LL NEVER GET ALL THIS TAR OUT BY MORNING! THE MUSEUM WILL CLOSE AND I'LL BE FORCED TO RESIGN!
HURRY! CAN'T YOU CLEAN UP ANY FASTER?

HMMM...REMINDS ME OF "THE CASE OF THE BOY AT THE BORDER" --EH, FREDDY?
IT SURE DOES, VELMA. AND NOW THIS CASE FINALLY MAKES SENSE!
LIKE, WHAT BOY? WHAT BORDER?
YOU SHOULD READ MORE DETECTIVE MAGAZINES LIKE ME AND FREDDY!
EVERY DAY, A BOY WOULD CROSS THE BORDER ON A BICYCLE WITH A SACK OVER HIS SHOULDER. THE BORDER POLICE CHECKED THE SACK EACH DAY-- BUT IT WAS JUST FULL OF SAND.
STILL, THEY WERE SURE HE WAS SMUGGLING SOMETHING ACROSS THE BORDER...
WELL, IF IT WAS A HOAX, THEY GOT OUR MOST VALUABLE PIECE--AND THEY GOT AWAY!
NOT QUITE-- STOP THESE WORKMEN!
I...I DON'T UNDERSTAND!
OH, DON'T YOU? WELL, LET US EXPLAIN!
THE TAR MONSTER WAS A PHONY--COOKED UP BY THE CURATOR AND HIS HENCHMEN!
HERE'S YOUR TAR MONSTER! THIS SNORKEL AND A LOT OF TAR--ENOUGH TO HIDE THE CURATOR!
HE WAS ABLE TO OOZE THROUGH THE RIB-CAGE, BECAUSE HE'S SKINNY--AND ALL THE REST WAS JUST SOFT TAR!

THE WHOLE THING WAS A SCAM TO COVER THE THEFT OF THE ARTIFACTS!
THE CURATOR HID THE OBJECTS IN THE TAR WHILE EVERYONE WAS RUNNING AROUND.
HE WASN'T COVERED IN TAR BECAUSE HE WAS ATTACKED BY THE MONSTER--BUT BECAUSE HE WAS THE MONSTER!
THE NEXT DAY, HIS HENCHMEN WOULD PICK UP THE STOLEN GOODS ALONG WITH THE "TAR MESS"--AND TAKE IT AWAY!
THEY WOULD HAVE GOTTEN AWAY WITH IT TOO, IF IT WEREN'T FOR THEIR GREED.
NOW WE'LL TAKE THEM AWAY!
YEAH, LIKE ALL THIEVES--THEY USED THE SAME SCAM UNTIL THEY GOT CAUGHT.
LIKE, WHAT DOES ALL THIS HAVE TO DO WITH A KID AND HIS BICYCLE?!
WELL, THE BOY STOPPED CROSSING THE BORDER. BUT ONE GUARD JUST HAD TO KNOW WHAT THE BOY HAD BEEN DOING, AND THE BOY TOLD HIM--
--HE'D BEEN SMUGGLING BICYCLES!
SO, HOW DOES THAT--WAIT?! THE CURATOR WAS STEALING BICYCLES?!
OH, SHAGGY!
HA HA HA
HA HA HA
THE END

PRISONER OF THE GHOST IN THE IRON MASK
NO ONE WILL MARRY THE PRINCESS! NO ONE!
WHERE'S A FAIRY GODMOTHER WHEN YOU NEED ONE?
ALEX SIMMONS • WRITER
LEO BATIC • PENCILS
HORATIO OTTOLINI • INKS
PAUL BECTON • COLORS
SNO CONE • SEPS
ROB LEIGH • LETTERS
HARVEY RICHARDS • ASST. EDITS
JOAN HILTY • EDITS
THIS IS YOUR END, PLAY ACTOR!
DON'T I AT LEAST GET A LAST MEAL--MAYBE FIVE OR SIX?
REAH! RAST REAL!
YOU SHOULD NEVER HAVE WOOED THE PRINCESS!
SEEMED LIKE A GOOD IDEA AT THE TIME!
EVEN THOUGH...

"...IT WASN'T MY IDEA."
PRINCESS ADORA, YOUR CASTLE-- IN FACT, YOUR WHOLE COUNTRY IS BEAUTIFUL!
LIKE YEAH, YOUR ROYALNESS. TOO BAD WE SPENT THE RIDE HERE HIDDEN IN A HAY WAGON.
SHAGGY!
I, TOO, AM SORRY YOU HAD TO BE SMUGGLED INTO MOROVANIA.
BUT IT WAS IMPERATIVE NO ONE KNEW THAT THE PRINCESS HAD HIRED... GHOST CHASERS. THAT IS WHY CAPTAIN MASONOV ARRANGED THINGS AS HE DID.
GHOST CHASERS! CHARLATANS, IS MORE LIKELY.
PRUCILLA!
THE REGENT IS RIGHT, AND THERE IS NO DENYING IT-- WE'VE ALL SEEN THE GHOST IN THE IRON MASK!
GHOST IN THE--!
WHO DO WE HAVE TO SEE TO GET SMUGGLED OUT OF HERE?
REAH!
TELL US MORE ABOUT THE GHOST, YOUR HIGHNESS.
THERE'S NOTHING TO TELL! IT'S JUST A--
THE LEGEND SAYS, MY DEAR COUSIN...THAT THE GHOST...

"...WAS ONCE A MAN NAMED KARL VON SAMO. HE CAME FROM A TOWN CALLED DONATALOT, AND WANTED TO MARRY THE PRINCESS OF THAT TIME.
"IT IS THE LAW OF OUR COUNTRY THAT THE PRINCESS CHOOSES THE MAN WHO WILL BE KING.
"SHE CARED FOR HIM TOO, BUT WAS HONOR BOUND TO MARRY A MAN OF ROYAL BLOOD. VON SAMO WAS NOT.
"WHEN SHE...REJECTED HIM, HE DISAPPEARED. SOME SAY HE WENT INTO THE FOREST. OTHERS CLAIM THE ROYAL COUNCIL LOCKED HIM AWAY IN THE DUNGEON.
"WHATEVER THE TRUTH, HE VANISHED UNTIL YEARS LATER, WHEN IT WAS TIME FOR THE QUEEN'S DAUGHTER TO CHOOSE A HUSBAND. THAT IS WHEN HE REAPPEARED...AS THE GHOST, WEARING AN IRON MASK.
"HE DROVE OFF ALL SUITORS, UNTIL THE QUEEN PLEADED WITH HIM. AFTER THAT, HE VANISHED.
"THAT PRINCESS WAS MY MOTHER."
NOW HE IS BACK.
OVER THE PAST FEW MONTHS, HE HAS DRIVEN OFF THREE OF MY SUITORS. EACH ONE WAS A PRINCE OF ROYAL BLOOD.
HE MUST BE STOPPED.
DON'T WORRY, YOUR HIGHNESS. WE'VE GOT A PLAN TO CATCH THIS GHOST.
ALL WE NEED IS THREE SERVANTS COSTUMES, AND...

"...AND ONE PRINCE OF A GUY."
HIS ROYAL HIGHNESS, PRINCE... uh, HAMONRYE, OF FOODONIA!
THIS IS FANTASTIC, FREAKY, SUPER!
REAH!
LIKE THERE'S ENOUGH FOOD HERE TO LAST...
RYVE RINNITS?
REMEMBER, YOU ARE SUPPOSED TO BE A PRINCE. BESIDES, THE GHOST MAY SHOW UP ANYWHERE, AT ANY TIME.
LIKE, DON'T WORRY, PRINCESS. WITH MYSTERY INC. ON THE JOB, AND ALL THESE GUARDS, WHAT CAN GO WRON--?
LOOK OUT, SCOOB!!!
YOU SHUNNED MY LOVE, REJECTED ME! SO...BE ALONE THROUGH ETERNITY!

WHAT'S THE USE? THEY'LL NEVER CATCH HIM.
AS BIG AS HE WAS, THAT MIGHT BE A GOOD THING!
POOF
MAYBE IT IS. IF THESE HAUNTINGS CONTINUE, I WON'T HAVE TO--
LIKE, HAVE TO WHAT?
OH, NEVER MIND!
I HOPE THE REST OF THE GANG COMES UP WITH SOME CLUES, SCOOB. BECAUSE I THINK THIS MYSTERY JUST GOT WEIRDER.
WE'VE LOST HIM.
IF IT'S A REAL GHOST, WHAT DOES HE GET OUT OF SCARING PRINCESS ADORA? REVENGE ON HER GRANDMOTHER?
THAT DOESN'T MAKE SENSE. HE LEFT THE LAST TIME BECAUSE THE QUEEN ASKED HIM TO. SO HE CAN'T STILL BE MAD AT HER.
BUT IF IT'S NOT A REAL GHOST... WHAT WOULD ANYONE GAIN BY DOING THIS?
I HEARD THE REGENT IS WORRIED HE'LL LOSE HIS INFLUENCE OVER THE ROYAL COUNCIL, ONCE PRINCESS ADORA BECOMES QUEEN.
AND THE SERVANTS TOLD ME COUSIN PRUCILLA IS NEXT IN LINE FOR THE THRONE, IF ADORA DOESN'T MARRY.
THAT'S TWO SUSPECTS AND MOTIVES, RIGHT THERE... IF THE GHOST ISN'T REAL!

OH, BUT I AM VERY REAL!
JINKIES! HOW'D HE GET BEHIND US?
RUN!
THAT'S A FRESH IDEA!
YOU CREPT INTO MY COUNTRY, MY HAUNTINGS TO STOP. INSTEAD YOU'VE FOUND...A PLACE TO ROT!
THERE YOU ARE, PRINCESS. LIKE, WHAT WERE YOU TALKING ABOUT DOWNSTAIRS?
I...I DO NOT WISH TO MARRY, NOT YET. NOT THIS WAY.
THERE ARE SO MANY THINGS I WANT TO DO FOR MY PEOPLE, ON MY OWN.
DO YOU HAVE TO GET MARRIED?

IT HAS BEEN THE LAW FOR GENERATIONS. THE PRINCESS MARRIES SOMEONE FROM ANOTHER KINGDOM TO HELP FORM STRONG BONDS BETWEEN OUR COUNTRIES.
IT IS OUR WAY...BUT IT IS SO UNFAIR!
RIT'S RA RHOST! RUN!!!
YOU CAST YOUR SORROW UPON THE AIR...
...BUT WHOEVER SAID THAT LIFE IS FAIR?
DID YOU NOTICE SOMETHING FUNNY ABOUT THE GHOST?
NOTHING ABOUT HIM IS FUNNY, EXCEPT HIS BAD POETRY!
HE SEEMED SMALLER TO ME JUST NOW. UPSTAIRS, HE LOOKED TALLER THAN ME. STRANGE.
HERE'S SOMETHING ELSE THAT'S STRANGE.
IT LOOKS LIKE IT WAS CARVED YEARS AGO.
"THEY'LL SET ME FREE TOMORROW AND HOME I WILL ROAM, TO LIVE MY DAYS WITHOUT HER, LOST AND...ALONE."

SO THEY *DID* LOCK UP VON SAMO DOWN HERE TO KEEP HIM AWAY FROM THE PRINCESS.
Hmmmmm... DIDN'T PRINCESS ADORA SAY THAT VON SAMO WAS FROM THE TOWN OF DONATALOT?
YES.
WELL, THE CASTLE PERSONNEL FILES SHOW THAT THERE'S SOMEONE ELSE FROM THAT TOWN...AND I THINK I KNOW WHO THE GHOST REALLY IS!
AND IF I'M RIGHT, WE'VE GOT TO GET TO SHAGGY AND THE PRINCESS BEFORE IT'S TOO LATE!
NOW PRINCESS, GIVE UP YOUR THRONE AND BE FREE TO DO WHAT YOU PLEASE!
NEVER!
NEVER IS A LONG TIME, MY PRINCESS FAIR. THIS I SHOULD KNOW! BUT IF FOREVER IS WHAT YOU WANT, I CAN TAKE YOU THERE!
COME ON, ***SCOOB!*** THIS IS NO TIME TO ***HANG*** OUT!

WE'VE GOT TO FIND THE GANG, SCOOB. BUT ONE OF US HAS TO HELP THE PRINCESS FIGHT OFF A FREAKY, SWORD-SWINGING GHOST!
ROOD RUCK RIT RA RHOST!
I FIGURED YOU'D SAY THAT.
NO PLACE TO RUN NOW, PRINCESS--AND NO ONE TO GUARD YOU.
WHERE ARE ALL THE GUARDS WHEN YOU NEED ONE? WELL... THIS WORKED IN ROBIN HOOD!
NOW LET'S RUN, PRINCESS!
ZOINKS! ANOTHER GHOST!
MY TRUSTY SWORD SAYS, YE SHALL NOT PASS. SO CHOOSE WELL YOUR WORDS. THEY'LL BE YOUR LAST!

GREAT WORK, SCOOBY! WHERE'S SHAGGY?
RIGHTING RA RHOST! RE REEDS RELP!
HE NEEDS HELP MORE THAN YOU KNOW, SCOOBY. 'CAUSE IF WE'RE RIGHT, HE'S NOT FIGHTING THE GHOST...
HE'S FIGHTING...
"...TWO OF THEM!"
LIKE, THIS IS TAKING A TWO-FOR-ONE SALE WAY TOO FAR!
ZOINKS!
RUN, PLAY ACTOR! RUN LIKE THE OTHERS DID BEFORE YOU!
I WAS NOT ONLY TRAINED TO GUIDE MY COUNTRY-- BUT ALSO TO FIGHT FOR IT!

HEADS UP, MR. GHOST...
GUESS YOU DIDN'T HAVE A LEG TO STAND ON.
YEOWWWW!
LOOKS LIKE SHAGGY AND THE PRINCESS ARE DOING DOUBLE-DUTY!
CRASH
THIS ROUND IS YOURS! BUT I'LL DIVE INTO THE MOAT AND MAKE MY ESCAPE!
HE WHO FIGHTS AND RUNS AWAY--
OWWWWW.
THE WINDOW OVERLOOKING THE MOAT...IS ON THE OTHER SIDE OF THE ROOM!

SO, KARL VON SAMO DID RETURN TO HIS VILLAGE, AND LATER HE MARRIED. THEIR SON ALWAYS FELT THAT HIS FATHER HAD BEEN CHEATED OF GREAT WEALTH AND POWER.
HE WANTED HIS DUE, SO HE CHANGED THE LETTERS IN HIS NAME. VON SAMO BECAME MASONOV. THEN HE CAME HERE AND JOINED THE PALACE GUARDS.
HE WORKED HIS WAY UP IN THE RANKS LOOKING FOR A WAY TO GET EVEN.
FINALLY, HE REALIZED HE COULD DO IT BY HELPING COUSIN PRUCILLA BECOME QUEEN.
PRUCILLA WOULD HAVE THE POWER, AND HE WOULD HAVE WEALTH AND REVENGE.
IT WOULD HAVE WORKED, TOO--
IF IT HADN'T BEEN FOR YOU MEDDLING KIDS!
PRINCESS, THESE EVENTS HAVE CAUSED SOME OF US TO RETHINK THE OLD LAWS. YOU ARE RIGHT. SOME CHANGES SHOULD BE MADE.
THEN IT SEEMS I HAVE MANY REASONS TO THANK MYSTERY INC.
ESPECIALLY SHAGGY, WHO SHOWED GREAT COURAGE WHERE THOSE OF ROYAL BLOOD RAN.
PERHAPS SOMEDAY YOU WILL MAKE A GOOD... THOUGH SOMEWHAT WEIRD RULER.
LIKE, THANKS, PRINCESS. BUT FOR NOW, IF I CAN'T BE A KING...
...LET ME AT LEAST DINE LIKE ONE! CHOW DOWN!
ROOBY ROOBY ROO!!!
THE END

THIS IS THE HOUSE OF AN EDGAR ALLAN POE FAN, ALL RIGHT! I CAN SEE WHY HE'D BE UPSET IF SOMEONE STOLE A COPY OF A TREASURED POE BOOK--HE SEEMS REALLY INTO THE CREEPY THINGS POE WROTE ABOUT!
NOT JUST A TREASURED BOOK, FREDDY--A HANDWRITTEN COPY OF POE'S EPIC POEM "THE RAVEN." THAT WOULD BE A STUNNING LOSS FOR ANY FAN OF LITERATURE!
IF IT'S MISSING FROM HERE, MAYBE A GHOST STOLE IT!
Cravin' the RAVEN
USHER
RURIK TYLER-writer • JOE STATON-penciller
ANDREW PEPOY-inker • NICK J NAP -letterer • SNO CONE-colorist
HARVEY RICHARDS-asst editor • JOAN HILTY-editor
IT IS NOT MISSING FROM HERE. I PLACED THE WINNING BID ON IT AT THE AUCTION HOUSE, BUT THE MANUSCRIPT WAS STOLEN BEFORE IT GOT HERE.
I'M EDGAR ALLAN JONES. I HIRED YOU TO FIND MY DOCUMENT. IT SHOULDN'T BE TOO DIFFICULT--I KNOW WHO STOLE IT!
IT'S NOT A GHOST, RIGHT?
NO. THIS IS A PICTURE OF ME PLACING THE WINNING BID. THIS WOMAN SEATED IN THE AUDIENCE--MISS LENORE--IS THE THIEF!
I DON'T KNOW...SHE LOOKS LIKE A GHOST TO ME!
THAT'S A STRONG ACCUSATION, MR. JONES. BUT LET'S GO PAY HER A VISIT!

SOON...
IT WOULDN'T BE A BAD IDEA TO ASK MISS LENORE, BUT WHY ARE YOU SO SURE SHE STOLE YOUR MANUSCRIPT?
SHE BID FURIOUSLY ALL DAY ON DIFFERENT POE ITEMS. SHE WAS OUTBID ON EVERY OBJECT, AND WENT HOME WITH NOTHING. I THINK SHE MUST HAVE GOTTEN SO DESPERATE THAT SHE WOUND UP STEALING SOMETHING!
AND SHE LIVES IN ANOTHER SPOOKY HOUSE? LIKE, WHO'S THIS TOWN'S REAL ESTATE AGENT-- DRACULA?
HELLO?
MISS LENORE, WE'RE MYSTERY INC. WE'D LIKE TO ASK YOU SOME QUESTIONS ABOUT THE MISSING "RAVEN" MANUSCRIPT...
MISSING?...
YES MISS LENORE, YOU STOLE IT--AND I'D LIKE IT BACK!
WHAT!!!!
HOW DARE YOU ACCUSE ME! LISTEN TO ME, JONES-- I WOULDN'T STEAL ANYTHING FROM YOU--AND YOU CAN JUST GET OUT OF MY HOUSE RIGHT NOW!
MISS LENORE, WE'D JUST LIKE TO ASK YOU SOME QUESTIONS...
THAT GOES FOR YOU TOO--GET OUT!!!

I DON'T SUPPOSE YOU COULD JUST HAVE THIS EDGAR ALLAN POE GUY WRITE YOU ANOTHER COPY, COULD YOU?
NOT VERY LIKELY--POE WAS FROM ANOTHER AGE, HE WAS *BORN* IN 1809!
GOTCHA-- HE'S PROBABLY TOO *TIRED* TO WRITE YOU ANOTHER COPY!
SHAGGY, HE'D BE CLOSE TO ***TWO HUNDRED YEARS OLD.***
MR. JONES, I DON'T KNOW MUCH ABOUT POE, OTHER THAN THAT HE WROTE SOME VERY SCARY STORIES. WHAT CAN YOU TELL US?
EDGAR ALLAN POE WAS A GREAT AMERICAN WRITER. HE WAS POVERTY-STRICKEN FOR MUCH OF HIS LIFE, BUT WHEN "THE RAVEN" WAS PUBLISHED IN 1845, HE AT LAST BEGAN TO GET SOME OF THE *RECOGNITION* HE DESERVED. TWO YEARS LATER, HIS WIFE DIED. HE WAS BROKENHEARTED. HE DISAPPEARED, AND NO ONE KNOWS WHAT THE LAST TWO YEARS OF HIS LIFE WERE LIKE. IT ISN'T EVEN KNOWN *WHAT* HE DIED OF-- SOME SAY DRINK, AND SOME SAY *RABIES!*
The Raven
THAT'S WHY I WANTED THE MANUSCRIPT SO BADLY. I LIKE TO THINK THE FAME IT BROUGHT HIM MADE HIM *HAPPY,* EVEN FOR A LITTLE WHILE.
IS THAT HIM? HE LOOKS JUST LIKE YOU!
THERE IS A RESEMBLANCE, I ADMIT--BUT POE NEVER NEEDED A *CANE.*

THERE'S ALL SORTS OF OTHER INFORMATION HERE IN MY COLLECTION.
WHO ARE THESE STATUES MODELLED AFTER?
LET'S SEE, THERE IS POE HIMSELF...FOLLOWED BY PALLAS...AND THAT IS LENORE.
Tales of the GROTESQUE and ARABESQUE
PALLAS ATHENA
EA POE
LENORE
MISS LENORE?
NO, NO-- LENORE IS A CHARACTER IN "THE RAVEN."
WELL, YOU'RE RIGHT-- THIS ANNOTATED COPY OF POE STORIES SURE HAS A LOT OF INFORMATION!
AND LIKE, WHAT'S WITH THE LITTLE DOLLHOUSES?
RUE MORGUE
THOSE ARE DIORAMAS I MADE OF SOME OF POE'S MORE FAMOUS STORIES...

THIS IS "THE TELL-TALE HEART." A CRAZY MAN THINKS HE CAN HEAR THE BEATING OF HIS VICTIM'S HEART. HE THINKS THE POLICE CAN HEAR IT TOO, AND THAT THEY KNOW ALL ABOUT HIS SECRET. THIS IS THE SCENE WHERE HE PULLS UP THE FLOORBOARDS TO REVEAL HIS HORRIBLE CRIME!
LIKE, LOOKS LIKE "THE TELL-TALE HOUSE REMODELER" TO ME!
THIS ONE SHOWS THE "CASK OF THE AMONTILLADO." ANOTHER NASTY LITTLE STORY ABOUT THE CRIMES OF A CRAZY MAN. HE LURES SOMEONE INTO A DEEP WINE CELLAR, PROMISING HIM FINE WINE, BUT INSTEAD WALLS HIM UP IN THE BRICKWORK FOREVER!
SOUNDS LIKE "RETURN OF THE TELL-TALE HOUSE RE-MODELER" TO ME! LIKE, IS POE THE GUY WHO DOES ALL THOSE TOOL COMMERCIALS ON TV?
MERLOT
THIS IS FROM POE'S NIGHTMARISH TALE OF THE SPANISH INQUISITION, "THE PIT AND THE PENDULUM"--WHERE A MAN IS THRUST INTO TOTAL DARKNESS, AND MUST AVOID A HUGE HOLE IN THE FLOOR, AND A GREAT SWINGING PENDULUM AX!
TOTAL DARKNESS, HUGE HOLE IN THE FLOOR, AND A LOOSE SWINGING AX--SOUNDS LIKE THIS GUY COULD USE A VISIT FROM THE "CRAZY HOUSE REMODELER"!
THAT'S SOME PRETTY FANCY WORK YOU'VE DONE THERE, MR. JONES.
I GOT THE IDEA FROM THE ONES AT THE AUCTION HOUSE--THEY'RE LIFE-SIZED!

MR. JONES, HOW CLOSELY WAS THE AUCTION HOUSE QUESTIONED ABOUT THE DISAPPEARANCE OF YOUR MANUSCRIPT?
THE POLICE CHECKED THE AUCTION HOUSE THOROUGHLY. THEY CHECKED THE WAREHOUSE, THE ARCHIVES, THE FILE CABINETS, THE OFFICES, AND THE STOCK ROOMS. "THE RAVEN" WAS NOT THERE.
THAT'S WHAT LED ME TO SUSPECT MISS LENORE--SHE WANTED THE MANUSCRIPT, AND NOW SHE HAS IT! I'M SURE OF IT!
The Raven
E.A. Poe
THESE BOOKS ARE GIVING ME SOME IDEAS. I SAY WE GO PAY A VISIT TO THE AUCTION HOUSE!
WELL, THEY'LL BE CLOSING SOON, SO IF WE'RE GOING, WE'D BETTER HURRY!
RET'S RO!
LIKE, CAN WE BID ON SOME SCOOBY SNACKS ON THE WAY?

YOU GUYS CAN HAVE ALL THE SCOOBY SNACKS YOU WANT--JUST STAY OUT OF MY WAY WHEN I TALK TO THE AUCTIONEER. I HAVE SOME IMPORTANT QUESTIONS TO ASK HIM!
THERE'S THE AUCTION HOUSE.
IT'S DARK-- DO YOU THINK THEY'RE ALREADY CLOSED?
LIKE, EITHER THAT, OR SOMEONE BID REALLY HIGH ON ALL THEIR LIGHT BULBS!
WAIT! SOMEONE WITH A FLASHLIGHT IS POKING AROUND ON THE SECOND FLOOR. WHAT COULD THAT MEAN?
THEY WANT TO BID ON THE FUSEBOX, TOO?
OR MAYBE ANOTHER ITEM IS GETTING STOLEN!

THESE ARE THE LIFE-SIZED DISPLAYS FROM POE'S STORIES? THEY'RE SURE CREEPY IN THE DARK.
IT MAKES ME WISH THE GUY HAD WRITTEN SOMETHING SAFE...LIKE COOKBOOKS!
OH SURE, THAT'S WHAT THE WORLD NEEDS--STORIES ABOUT CRAZY CHEFS BATTER-DIPPING EVERYBODY, AND THEN BAKING THEM IN CAKES FOREVER AND EVER...
LOOK! WHAT'S THAT?!
OH MY GOSH, ISN'T THAT MISS LENORE?
LIKE, IT'S HARD TO TELL, FREDDY--SHE ISN'T YELLING AT ANYBODY!
OBVIOUSLY SHE'S COME TO STEAL SOMETHING ELSE! SEE? WHAT DID I TELL YOU?!
EASY NOW...LET'S GO ASK HER WHAT SHE'S UP TO!
FROM THE LOOKS OF THINGS, I'D SAY SHE'S PRACTICING TO BE A GHOST!
SHAGGY, THAT'S SILLY.
MAYBE SO, BUT IF SHE STARTS WALKING THROUGH WALLS, I'M OUT OF HERE!

MISS LENORE! WAIT A SECOND!
OOOH-- YOU SCARED ME!
WE SCARED YOU!? YOU'RE THE ONE WHO LOOKS LIKE A GHOST!
WHAT ARE YOU DOING HERE, MISS LENORE? LOOKING FOR SOMETHING ELSE TO STEAL?
I CAME HERE TO CLEAR MY NAME! AND, IF YOU MUST KNOW--TO GET THE MANUSCRIPT BACK TO ITS RIGHTFUL OWNER-- YOU! IF THAT CAN'T BE ME, THEN IT CERTAINLY SHOULDN'T BE SOME CROOK!
YOU BID ON THAT MANUSCRIPT FAIR AND SQUARE, JONESY, AND IT IS AN OUTRAGE THAT YOU DON'T HAVE IT!
YOU...UHM... I..ER...
MISS LENORE, WHAT DO YOU THINK OF THIS?
POE
YES! THAT IS IMMEDIATELY WHAT I THOUGHT OF! BUT I CHECKED THE POE DISPLAYS, AND THE MANUSCRIPT ISN'T THERE. THAT'S WHY I CAME TO THE ALICE IN WONDERLAND DISPLAYS...

WHAT'S WITH THE BIG RABBIT? DID POE WRITE SOME WEIRD KIND OF WOLFMAN STORY?
POE DIDN'T WRITE ALICE IN WONDERLAND. LEWIS CARROLL DID.
THAT'S A RELIEF-- LEWIS CARROLL DIDN'T WRITE ANY WEIRD KIND OF WOLFMAN STORY, DID HE?
BE QUIET, SHAGGY, WE'RE TRYING TO SEE...
THAT'S ENOUGH! WHAT IS THE MEANING OF THIS?
SOMEONE SPOTTED US!
IT'S THE AUCTIONEER!
I SHALL CALL THE POLICE!
GOOD! CALL THE POLICE! THEY CAN ARREST YOU! YOU'RE THE ONE WHO STOLE THE MANUSCRIPT-- IT'S RIGHT HERE ON THE WALL!
THAT'S RIDICULOUS-- YOU MUST ALL BE OUT OF YOUR MINDS!
LOOK OUT!!!
SWOOSH
AHHHHHHH!

GOT IT!
CLANG
OH, THANK GOODNESS-- IT'S ONLY RUBBER! I WAS AFRAID FOR A SECOND THERE THAT YOU WERE GOING TO BE HURT.
I...UHM ...ERR...
NOT SO FAST, YOU SCOUNDREL!
OOOOFF!
GOODNESS! I'M SO GLAD YOU HAD THAT CANE WITH YOU!
FOR THE FIRST TIME IN MY LIFE, SO AM I. MISS LENORE, I...I WANT YOU TO HAVE THE MANUSCRIPT.
THAT'S A VERY GALLANT OFFER...EDGAR.
PLEASE... CALL ME JONESY.
I SAY YES...JONESY... BUT ONLY IF IT MEANS YOU'LL COME VISIT IT...EVERY DAY.
ROW ROMANRIC!
The Raven

SHORTLY AFTERWARD...
VELMA, WHAT CLUE WERE YOU AND MISS LENORE TALKING ABOUT?
IT WAS IN THE BOOK!
POE
EDGAR ALLAN POE INVENTED THE DETECTIVE SHORT STORY--AND ONE OF HIS MOST FAMOUS WAS "THE PURLOINED LETTER"! THAT WAS A STORY WHERE A LETTER THAT WAS EMBARRASSING TO THE QUEEN FALLS INTO THE WRONG HANDS. THE POLICE THINK THEY HAVE THE RIGHT SUSPECT, BUT A SEARCH OF HIS HOUSE TURNS UP NOTHING. IT TURNS OUT HE HID THE LETTER BY FRAMING IT AND HANGING IT ON THE WALL--IN PLAIN SIGHT! IT WAS UNDER THE NOSES OF THE POLICE THE WHOLE TIME!
THE AUCTIONEER DID THE SAME THING WITH THE MISSING MANUSCRIPT!
AND IT LOOKS LIKE YOU'LL BE STEALING FROM YOUR CUSTOMERS...
...NEVER-MORE! SQUAWK!
HA HA HA HA HA HA
HA HA
MEDDLING KIDS!
THE END.

SKRRRRAWK!!!!
FREDDIE! HIT THE BRAKES!
IT'S THE JERSEY DEVIL!
OOF! EASY, SNEEZY! WE'RE GETTING SCRAMBLED LIKE BOP AND REBOP BACK HERE!
SKREEEEEEEEE
THE JERSEY DEVIL
TERRENCE GRIEP JR.- WRITER
JOE STATON- PENCILS
DAVE HUNT- INKS
RYAN CLINE- LETTERER
DIGITAL CHAMELEON- COLORIST
HARVEY RICHARDS- ASST EDITOR
JOAN HILTY- EDITOR

BONK
THE MYSTERY MACHINE
WELL, IT *WAS* THE JERSEY DEVIL...
NOW IT'S...
...A REALLY BIG TREE...
ON A REALLY, REALLY STEEP CLIFF!!!
BIG TREE. STEEP CLIFF. GOT IT.
SPLITCH
ZOINKS...
JINKIES...
YEESH, YOU GUYS REALLY *ARE* SCRAMBLED!
SKRRRAWK
WE'RE SAFE NOW...BUT THE JERSEY DEVIL IS ESCAPING!
HOW DARE YOU TRY TO SCARE MY DETECTIVES AWAY, YOU...YOU... *LIABILITY,* YOU!
FAMILY CURSE OR NO, I'M STILL PUTTING THIS FESTIVAL ON, BLAST YOU!

LOOKS LIKE YOU GUYS COULD USE A *HAND*.
ACTUALLY, LIKE, I COULD USE SOME *FOOD* TO SETTLE MY STOMACH!
I'M *DONALD LEEDS*, CEO OF LEEDS ENTERPRISES. THANKS FOR COMING, KIDS.
THAT *FIEND* IS THE REASON YOU'RE HERE. IT'S CUTTING INTO MY *PROFIT MARGINS!*
AH-*HEM!*
OH, AND THIS IS MY *KITE DESIGNER*, QUINCY PALLUS LEEDS. SHE'S GOING TO BE THE MICHELANGELO OF WIND ART!
AND I'M ALSO HIS *DAUGHTER*. CALL ME Q.P.
SO THAT *WINGED GREMLIN* IS YOUR PROBLEM, MR. LEEDS?
IS IT EVER! THE *JERSEY DEVIL* IS...
BREE EEP
EXCUSE ME... ENTREPRENEURSHIP BECKONS!
JAMAL, HELLO. HOW GOES THE CONCESSION STAND? I'M IN A MEETING... MM? NO, NO, I CAN *MULTITASK*...
HEY, SCOOBERT, DIG THAT CRAZY CELL PHONE! I BET WE CAN ORDER *TAKEOUT!*
SMEK
BOTTOM LINE, KIDS: LEEDS ENTERPRISES IS HOSTING THE JERSEY KITE FESTIVAL, AND QUINCY'S *NEWEST DESIGN* WILL BE IN...
...THE DEEP FRYERS.
E-EXCUSE US...?

SORRY; TALKING TO JAMAL. WHAT ABOUT THE DEEP FRYERS, JAMAL?
DEEP FRYERS? COOL! LIKE, THIS CASE WILL BENEFIT FROM OUR SKILLS, SCOOB!
WE WON LAST YEAR'S KITE FESTIVAL WITH A KITE I DESIGNED; SO OF COURSE DAD HAD TO GO INTO THE KITE BUSINESS...
AND THEN THINGS REALLY TOOK FLIGHT. LEEDS ENTERPRISES IS SPONSORING THE FESTIVAL THIS YEAR!
HERE'S THIS YEAR'S MODEL, THE WHITE ANGEL. BIG WHOOP.
LISTEN TO HER...SO MODEST! THE WHITE ANGEL IS BLUE-CHIP STOCK, QUINCY...
...BUT IF THE WHITE ANGEL'S DEBUT FLOPS, LEEDS ENTERPRISES WILL BE FRIED.
RO RAND RO'S! RROOVY!
...NO, JAMAL, NOT YOU.
SO KITE-FLYING IS A FAMILY AFFAIR, IS IT?
THAT'S NOT THE ONLY FAMILY AFFAIR CAUSING PROBLEMS.
WE'RE OPERATING UNDER THE LIABILITY OF A FAMILY CURSE!

IN COLONIAL TIMES, A WITCH NAMED MOTHER LEEDS--OUR ANCESTOR, I'M AFRAID--CALLED UPON THE FORCES OF DARKNESS AND CONJURED...
...THE JERSEY DEVIL!
THAT'S JUST AN URBAN LEGEND, DAD...
"OH? IS IT JUST AN 'URBAN LEGEND' THAT, OVER THE YEARS, HAS BEEN SEEN BY HUNTERS, FARMERS, POLICE OFFICERS AND EVEN CITY COUNCILMEN?
"WAS IT JUST AN URBAN LEGEND THAT, ONE WEEK IN JANUARY 1909...
"...WAS REPORTED BY THOUSANDS FROM BRISTOL TO TRENTON?
"THESE SIGHTINGS ARE DOCUMENTED FACT. THINK WHAT YOU WILL, BUT ALL THOSE PEOPLE SAW SOMETHING.
"WAS IT JUST AN URBAN LEGEND THAT HAS TORN TO SHREDS EVERY ONE OF THE WHITE ANGEL'S TEST FLIGHTS?
"WE WERE CONDUCTING ONE WHEN YOU YOUNG DETECTIVES ARRIVED..."
WHAT? JAMAL, WHAT'S OVERFLOWING? QUINCY, WILL YOU SHOW OUR INVESTIGATORS AROUND? I'VE GOT TO SEE TO THIS PERSONALLY. PLEASANT MEETING YOU.
MM? NO, JAMAL, I DEFINITELY WASN'T TALKING TO YOU...
AH, LISTEN... I'LL SHOW YOU YOU LEEDS MANOR.

JUST LIKE DAD SPENDS MOST OF HIS TIME ON THAT PHONE--TRYING TO OUTTALK THE "FAMILY CURSE"--I SPEND MOST OF MY TIME IN MY ROOM.
KLIK
LIKE, YOU CRASH HERE? MAN, THIS PAD IS THE *PADDEST!*
OR I'M IN THE *VAULT*...THAT'S MY WORKSHOP AND IT'S WHERE WE KEEP THE BLUEPRINTS FOR THE WHITE ANGEL.
HERE YA GO, LITTLE GOATEE.
AS YOU CAN SEE, I'VE EVEN GOT THE PET MONKEY I'D ALWAYS WANTED, SHAGGY. HIS NAME IS CRITTER.
HEY!
OO-OO!
YEAH, IT'S A GREAT LIFE, ALL RIGHT. BUT I'D GIVE IT ALL UP...
CHEE-CHEE!
...JUST TO GO FLYING KITES WITH MY DADDY AGAIN.
UH...WELL, UH, THAT CAN'T HAPPEN UNTIL WE GROUND THIS MYSTERY, SO...
LET'S SPLIT UP, GANG.
SHAGGY, SCOOBY AND YOU SEARCH THE *TEST GROUNDS*. SEE IF YOU CAN PICK UP THE DEVIL'S TRAIL. WE'LL EXPLORE THE *HOUSE* WITH Q.P.
SIGH.

SOON...
HEY, MAYBE YOU SHOULD CHECK THE ATTIC FOR CLUES TOO. WE HAVEN'T BEEN THERE YET...
THANKS FOR THE GRAND TOUR, Q.P., BUT WE'VE BEEN SOLVING MYSTERIES FOR A WHILE NOW...I THINK THE VAULT IS THE FIRST PLACE WE SHOULD HAVE SEARCHED.
...AND IF THESE BLUEPRINTS ARE AS VALUABLE AS YOUR FATHER THINKS THEY ARE, WE'VE GOT TO VERIFY THAT...THAT...
...WHAT AM I SEEING THERE?
CREEAAK
THE JERSEY DEVIL! AND HE HAS THE BLUEPRINTS!
SKRRRAWWWW!!!
HANG TIGHT, GANG! I'LL TACKLE HIM!
WELL, IF YOU'RE THE TACKLE, THEN I'LL PLAY BACKUP!
SPLOOT
HYOOLP!
OOPS. SORRY.
QUICK! WE'VE GOT TO GET THOSE BLUEPRINTS BACK, AND THE JERSEY DEVIL IS HEADING FOR...

"...THE TEST GROUNDS!"
THOSE DEEP-FRYERS SOUNDED AWFULLY SUSPICIOUS TO MY EXPERTLY-TRAINED EAR, SCOOBY. WHAT SAY WE START BY INVESTIGATING THAT CONCESSION STAND?
DUCK? LIKE, I WAS THINKING MORE ALONG THE LINES OF CHEESE CURDS...
RHAGGY! RUCK!
NUH-UH! NUH-UH! RUCK! RUCK--!
WHOOOOSH
WELL, J-JIG MY WIG!
OW! HEY! WE'RE LANDIN' IN THAT UN-ROUND BREEZE BOX!
AND SAID BREEZE BOX IS...
RUH--
BREEZING!
ROOBY ROOBY ROOOOOO!

LIKE, YOU KNOW WHAT WOULD SOUND BETTER THAN A DIZZY GILLESPIE SOLO RIGHT NOW, SCOOB?
RUT?
AN UPDRAFT!
COME ON, EVERYONE! THERE GOES THE JERSEY DEVIL! MAYBE WE COULD GRAB THE WHITE ANGEL AND...
TOO LATE, FREDDIE. LOOK...
SHAGGY AND SCOOBY HAVE HITCHED A RIDE ON THE WHITE ANGEL! BUT WITH THE JERSEY DEVIL UP THERE...
"...WHO'S CHASING WHOM?"
WELL, WE GOT THAT UPDRAFT, OLD PAL. BUT NOW WE'VE GOT A BIGGER PROBLEM...
LIKE, I DON'T SEE THE CONCESSION STAND ANYWHERE!
REVIL, RHAGGY--!

GREAT WHISTLIN' OCARINAS!
RIPE-RIPE-RIIIPE!
I THINK IT WAS SIR ISAAC NEWTON WHO SAID, "GRAVITY, MAN, WHAT A DRAG!"
WELL, I'M BACK!
SAY, WOULD YOU KIDS MIND SIGNING SOME FORMS BEFORE CONTINUING YOUR INVESTIGATION? I DON'T WANT ANY MESSY LAWSUITS IF...
THIS IS NO TIME TO TALK BUSINESS, MR. LEEDS!
SCOOBY-DOO, WHERE ARE YOOOOOO?
CRASH
SO, THERE'S SHAGGY, AND THERE'S THE JERSEY DEVIL, BUT WHERE'S...?
SCOOBY!
ROOBY-ROOBY-ROO-OO!

BUT WHAT ABOUT THE JERSEY DEVIL? IS HE A ROBOT, OR...?
WELL, WHILE I'M HANGIN' AROUND HERE...
CRITTER!
B-BUT... HOW?
HMMM...MAYBE Q.P.'S "ACCIDENTAL" INTERFERENCE AT THE VAULT WASN'T ALL THAT ACCIDENTAL...
QUINCY! IS THAT TRUE?
I... YEAH.
I DESIGNED THAT COSTUME AND TRAINED CRITTER TO FLY IT. HE "SCREAMS" THANKS TO MY COMPUTERS AND A HIDDEN CD PLAYER.
THEN... I HAD HIM STEAL MY OWN BLUEPRINTS.
I DON'T BELIEVE THIS, QUINCY! AFTER ALL I'VE DONE TO BUILD A BUSINESS FOR US...AND RID US OF THE FAMILY CURSE...!!!
BREE-EEP
BREE-EEP
THAT'S JUST IT, DAD!
THE ONLY WAY TO GET THROUGH TO YOU ANYMORE IS THROUGH YOUR BUSINESS! SO I "CAPITALIZED" ON YOUR SUPERSTITION WHILE PRE-TENDING NOT TO BELIEVE IN IT!
BREE-EEP
BREE-EEP

I...I DON'T WANT TO BE THE MICHELANGELO OF WIND ART, DAD. I JUST...
...I JUST WANT TO BE YOUR DAUGHTER AGAIN.
BREE-EEP
BREE-EEP
I SUPPOSE THE ONLY REAL FAMILY CURSES WE BEAR ARE...THE ONES WE DESIGN OURSELVES.
YOUNG MAN...YOU SEEMED TO, EH, DIG THIS PHONE WHEN WE MET. WELL...IT'S FOR YOU.
SMAK
BREE-EEP
BREE-EEP
TURNS OUT I'VE GOT A MORE *IMPORTANT* APPOINTMENT.
WITH Q.P.
NOW IF YOU'LL EXCUSE ME...
...I'VE GOT TO GO FLY A KITE.
YO, JAMAL? THIS IS MR. LEEDS'S... AH...NEW *ASSISTANT*. WHICH WAY TO THE *CONCESSION STAND?*
HA HA HA HA HA HA
12
THE END

CREATURE FEATURES!!
SCOOBY-DOO!
& THE HAUNTED HOUSE
ISBN: 1 84023 832 1
SCOOBY-DOO!
& THE CREEPY CRUISE
ISBN: 1 84023 884 4
SCOOBY-DOO!
& THE MUMMY MYSTERY
ISBN: 1 84023 977 8
OUT NOW!

THE POWERPUFF GIRLS™
THE POWERPUFF GIRLS
Go, Girls, Go!
ISBN: 1 84023 885 2
THE POWERPUFF GIRLS
To The Rescue!
ISBN: 1 84023 886 0
ALL SWEETNESS AND MIGHT...
SOON